Lanterns of the Lost

A Novella

Rixi Hazelwood

Lanterns of the Lost by Rixi Hazelwood

Copyright © 2022 Rixi Hazelwood

Cover by Eliushi from @eliushi.draws

For everyone whose kindness and support helped light my path along the way

CHAPTER 1

The Last Pathmaster

The Shores of Separation are quiet as Dennira starts her day. It's just the way she likes it, not that she has any choice in the matter. The sweet smell of souls drifts down from the iridescent current high above. There's a lot of traffic up there today, and with a haughty smile she delights in reminding herself that those souls are no longer her concern. They are beautiful to gaze at though, during those days and nights when the sting of her loneliness is the most keen.

The terrain of the desolate island would be tricky for some, but not for Dennira. She can walk around it with her eyes closed, and in a way she does. The blindfold doesn't bother her. She stopped noticing it years ago. To most it would look like a regular blindfold, but Dennira knows better.

It's a comfort more than anything, knowing what it keeps at bay. The smooth, black cloth doesn't block sight, but magic. It turns her view of the world dull and human.

If she can't use her power for its purpose, then she won't use it at all.

The bright, layered colours and secrets of the ancient pact she once held would only be a reminder of all she's lost. Better to cover them. A single strip of dark cloth holding the balance between sanity and ruin.

The cloven hooves at the end of her slender legs navigate the paths with ease. She tends the tracks well, but at the back of the island where the path to the lanterns lies among the jagged rock, it isn't so simple. Unless you're a native, you wouldn't even know the path through the rocks was there at all.

With an ironic and bitter chuckle that comes out as more of a huff, she supposes that maybe she's still a pathmaster of sorts after all. She pushes the thought away, imagining it floating up to join the current of souls above. Out of sight, out of mind.

Her silver staff is etched with intricate carvings and makes the trek around the island smoother. It comes level with the top of her head, straight until it curves into an elegant question mark gilded with small sculptures. Hanging from the underside of the crook is a petite bell made of the same metal. It tinkles while she walks, the sound feeding information back to her from all around the shores. Below it a dancing flame passes through all the shades of blue that have ever existed. Her constant companion and the endless light of her kin.

Starting at the back of the island is more a matter of practicality than anything else. Her home, hidden high up on the cliffs, is marked by the most ornate lantern. The one whose company she prefers. She'd never tell the others that but they probably know. From up on the cliffs the path is always the same. There's only so much variation to island life. It isn't a sprawling place, but it's large enough to have once housed a population of nearly two-hundred of her kind with plenty of space to spare.

Her gaze tracks her route. From the cliffs down to their base, then back up a steep climb that leads to a rolling grass plain clotted with forest and wild brush. These wilds dwindle into a flatter landscape littered with smaller copses of trees. The settlement isn't discernible anymore, and Dennira has no intention of looking for it among the tangle of nature and memories.

Her raven hair, sleek and shining under the ever-changing lights of the soul currents, hangs down her back in a straight and glossy sheet. Half of it is down, but the top half is scraped back out of her face and fastened in a braided bun just above the tight knot of the blindfold. Two plaits fall over her graceful shoulders, starting in front of her broken antlers and coming to rest just above her bust. The dark of her hair and blindfold are stark against her alabaster complexion and the fine grey fur of her lower half.

Some might say her fur is silver like her staff, but it's

mostly hidden by the folds of her midnight blue dress cloak, which brushes against the moss-strewn ground with a whisper yet never seems to impede her progress. It parts at the waist under a thick leather belt, and reveals a black dress with a skirt that hems where a human's knee would be. And so her daily round begins again.

The lanterns whisper to her as she touches the warm fire of her staff to each of them, replenishing their light and vitality. She revels in their ephemeral company for the short time her flame summons the spirits within them closer to the physical plain. Conversing and sharing memories with them. Some she's closer to than others, some she misses desperately, but all deserve to have their lantern kept alight. When it became her sole purpose Dennira isn't exactly sure. After all, how easy is it to remember anything when you spent decades in darkness roaming what was once a very different home than the ruins you're left with?

No, don't think on it now. Keep it at bay. The wave of memories rises and threatens to crash against her as the sheer rock starts to turn to flora-edged paths. They don't deserve to be responsible for any more distress.

But the burning hate will always be there, simmering away for eternity somewhere deep in Dennira's being. A different kind of flame to the one that nurtures the memory of her lost kin. A scorching, blistering orange blaze full of foul-smelling despair and mottled loss.

It burns like incense, strong enough to send sparks through a matted network of thorny and negative desires. Ones she won't give in to. Ones she can't let out. Harbour them and keep them down. Trample them and remind yourself. You are Dennira. You are alone only when the lanterns lose their light.

The last pathmaster does not take nutrition from the hate of wretched humans. No, they have been left in the dark, unattached to these shores. Cut off from millenniums of traditional guidance because of their ignorance and grief. Because of a single mistake. They have no place here, not even in her thoughts.

The storm passes as the spirit of the next lantern reminds her to collect particular herbs on her way home.

'Yes, of course I'll remember. And yes I'll make sure to hang them to dry out in the light of the gold moon next week. Even now you must miss your work to insist on reminding me of these details so many decades later, Jennir. Yes, yes, I'll harvest the crystal herbs soon too, I promise.' A joyful laugh echoes in Dennira's mind in response, and for a second the flame caresses her cheek as though it were the gentle hand of the island's most meticulous apothecary. She presses into it and the pressure holds. A deep ache in her chest tries to fight its way forward.

If there's a herb growing on this island, possibly on this plain or any of the ones beyond it, Jennir knows all its names, uses and the correct and most efficient way to prepare it. The days spent in Jennir's hut are an education Dennira can never repay her for, not now. The flare of each spirit lasts a few minutes, and on the whisper of its retreat comes praise bursting with pride that spreads across Dennira's face in a reminiscent smile. 'Thank you.'

Dennira knows exactly how many lanterns are on the island, and doesn't count them as she visits anymore. Why assign a number to the loss? It only makes it greater. A breeze rustles through the forest as she makes her way down, longing to end the first half of her lap on the beach staring out onto the inky sea. Only looking, never entering. No.

The water is home to many things. Very few would thank you for causing disturbance. You'll likely pay with your life or some piece of yourself. Here and there along the path she stops, clipping herbs, flowers and grasses. She stores them in various leather pouches or liquid-filled bottles that appear in her hand with a sweep or tap of her staff, and vanish just as easily. Never carry with you what you can summon with your skills.

The next lantern is adorned with blue-eyed moths. They can grow to the size of lilypads, but often leave the island long before they reach such a size. They are docile creatures, feeding on the flame of her staff or the lanterns on occasion as though it were pollen vital to their existence. Sometimes she wonders if it's the flame that turns their eyes blue and produces the wonderful, glittering networks of cobalt capillaries on their otherwise night-coloured wings.

When they do mature and claim their freedom, their blue patterning turns a brilliant gold. It's a comforting thought to believe that maybe, just maybe, these creatures take pieces of her kins' essence with them when they leave the island. Take them on one last adventure. Whether it's true or not matters little, it brings a warm swell to Dennira's chest to believe it.

She lights the lantern and moves on, catching wind of an urgent plea from a lantern back up on the cliffs.

She gently blows a moth from its perch on her finger and quickens her pace. Lanterns only reach out on the wind when something is wrong. She'll have to replenish the rest later, they have plenty of life left in them yet.

Dennira reaches the lantern near her home quickly and breathless.

'Annika… what? What is it?' Her head swivels towards the beach, her skilled eyes scanning and an unfriendly scowl adorning her face. She just came from near there, but there's more than a good reason to hurry back as she sees what troubles Annika's spirit. 'Let's hope you're wrong. This is no place for filth.'

She strokes and thanks the lantern and collects herself before leaping back down the path. Her robe billows in her haste. Scowl turning to a sneer.

Her posture becomes stiff, and she holds her staff ready for use without mercy. They dare keep sending their kind here? What more can they take? She'll add to her kill count if needed. No one can call it unreasonable.

CHAPTER 2

Alone and Unsure

Dark colours part as her senses return one at a time. The cold comes first, its spikey touch skittering over her skin. The damp kind no one enjoys. Something crunches against her face like gristle, and grinds between her teeth. Sand isn't usually so coarse, not on the beaches at home. She crossed successfully, then.

There's no stinging smell of salt. If she's on a beach shouldn't that be a given? The thick lapping of water reaches her ears. Why is there no salt in the sea? Her limbs creak with stiffness, as though she's wearing heavy denim on every inch of herself.

Another sound slinks into her perception. Sticky and wet. It moves from her neck and up towards her ear, squirming and swirling as it goes. The flickering of it right over her ear is enough to jumpstart her nervous system, and she thrusts herself up into a kneeling position with both arms. Flapping a hand over her ear and sending a spray of the strange sand into the air. She must have imagined it, but it sounded gross.

A dull headache slips across her uncharacteristically

calm mind as it reboots one layer at a time. Carrying her out of the depths and into cognition again. Where is she? What's she doing here? Where's here? The questions stir in a bracing wind as she tests the movement of her limbs. She's alive, and not really hurt, just confused.

Strange smells tinge the air, a different air than she's used to breathing. It's layered with the unknown, but it fills her lungs and exits them without trouble. Spreading her hands wide in front of her newly unblurred eyes she sees that the grains of sand aren't sand at all, not really. They're bigger, and more condensed. Sturdy even, like tiny, perfectly clear gemstones.

The shadowed water laps at the shore. A beach afterall. She's been unceremoniously flung on to the shores of a weird beach. Marvellous. Panic blows in on the next gust to roll off the gelatinous sea, but the steady words of her father are there as a constant reminder. How do we handle panic, Kyra? We think about what we know for sure.

So Kyra straightens her back, shaking the excess grains from her hair. Its soft corkscrew curls trying to cling to them. It will take forever to brush them all out. Taking a deep breath she pulls her ebony locks up into a high ponytail. She can sort it later, she needs to focus now. With her hair out of her face and no longer clinging to her neck and shoulders like gentle clouds, Kyra sets about working out what she knows for sure.

14

She's on a beach. Not a normal one but a beach all the same. That means she managed to travel successfully. It's a place where the sea meets the sand. The sky is deeper than the sky back home. Things ripple through it. Layers of ink-flooded water being stirred by some unseen paintbrush. Why isn't the one at home more like it? She prefers this one. It's more beautiful. Focus, Kyra, focus. You have to control the questions or you'll never get anywhere. There are no other islands nearby. Every direction is open water and emptiness.

The water is dangerous. She doesn't know why, but she knows that much is true. Warning crackles through it. Fizzes over its surface. A jolt of relief that she didn't land any closer to it gallops across her heart. Escaping with only one half-soaked jean leg where an errant wave must have spilled over her as she lay sprawled and semi-conscious. This is an island. A lone island in the middle of nowhere.

Details slide into place but don't quite click. She's meant to be here, she was sent. Well, volunteered. There's an important reason. Something she came to fetch and take home. Something difficult to find. It will come back to her eventually. Travelling to other plains often leaves people a bit muddled, it's Kyra's least favourite part of the process by far. Another thrum of aches ripple over her mind. Give it time, Kyra. Let yourself settle. Keep gathering information.

15

There are cliffs, tall and daunting, at the back of the island. Well, it might not be the back but who's to say what the front is? It's the back to Kyra and so that's what she's going with. It only seems right that she considers herself appearing at the front door instead of sneaking in through the back uninvited.

She's uninvited either way, she realises. Who has she disturbed, if anyone? The beach meets grassland and rises into copses, and further back a thick forest meets the base of the network of jagged rock. Could anyone live here? Was it even possible? Stop with the questions. What's something else you know? She's alone. Alone and unsure. It hits hard. Her purpose lost in the stuttering of her own mind which seems as structured as the bizarre sky above. Stand up, keep going. Something will come up.

It's a bigger effort to stand than expected, but she manages with a sigh. A shiver stops her. Drifting in off the quiet but somehow restless sea. Her feet crunch in the sand as she turns with a sharp and guarded motion. Nothing. Just endless landscapes changing on the surface every second.

A hypnotic shadow hisses in the depths. Whispers her name. Pulls on her core. Rolls it around with its beckoning. Back and forth it undulates. A careful lure. Dancing just for her. Lure being the operative word, Kyra. Lure. You're not bait. No, there's no shadow.

That would be creepy. We don't do creepy, we do practical. Stay practical.

'State your purpose or leave. This is no place for filth.'

Kyra yelps with surprise, becoming tangled in her own knees as she tries to whirl back, and ends up kneeling in the sand again looking up at her inquisitor. Who is she? What is she? Does she live here? Of course she must live here why else would she be here? The creature sounds unfriendly, and familiarity chimes again like a gong. It's something to do with why she's here. All at once words fail Kyra. Melding together in the furnace of her shock and confusion.

The woman-esque person is pale. Paler than anyone Kyra's ever seen. Is she sick? Dying? Made of porcelain? The questions tumble to a bottleneck and push against her vocal chords in a clamouring stampede to be the first out. If a human of average proportions had been remoulded and stretched, and had both their legs replaced with those of a silver deer, they might look a little like this creature. Not quite a centaur, for she only has two legs. Not quite a faun from the fairytales. She's too svelte and has too much gentle grace.

Grace that isn't reflected in her expression. Blindfolded but grimacing. If the creature's eyes were unveiled Kyra knows she'd feel the burn of hate. She's seen it in humans before. This creature doesn't need eyes to make the hatred burn though. It pours off her in pulses. Her antlers are small, possibly even dainty if they weren't so clearly broken.

'I asked your purpose. Answer me.'

Come on Kyra, stop staring and say something. By the look of this creature your life may well depend on it.

CHAPTER 3

Some Other Kind of Magic

A human girl. On Dennira's shores. She's got some nerve coming here. Are they regrouping? Planning to send more once this one scouts the situation and feeds information back? Dennira's body aches with the tension of trying not to attack. The girl is stunned, floundering in her fear. Good. She should be afraid.

'Don't make me ask again, or my staff will be your answer.'

Still she says nothing. Working her mouth to no avail. Her presence is chaotic and curious. Nothing like the solid, one-track purpose of the humans who landed here that day. She can't be more than eighteen. You see enough humans and you become good at guessing ages. That, and her soul reads young. It's still growing into itself, defining itself, exploring.

Seeing souls this young on the shores used to be a saddening thing. No, the past can't creep in now. She must focus on getting this filth off her beach.

Seconds tick by and finally the girl manages to speak.

'Hi there, sorry you startled me. I don't mean any harm, but I'm not quite sure where I am. Don't suppose you'd help me out on that front?' A nervous laugh stutters through her tight smile. Dennira's knuckles turn a pale pink around her staff. The light and carefree tone of voice slaps against her as though she's the butt of a joke. Her teeth grind together. How dare this human come here with such a casual and haughty tone.

'State your purpose.'

The girl's cordial smile vanishes. Cut away by Dennira's scathing intonation. Always assume the worst of them. Every time. They'll try all sorts of tricks to lower your guard, but not this time.

'I uhhh… my purpose. I'm sorry but… I'm a bit fuzzy on that too. I'm sure it'll come back to me, just a well-known side-effect of travel… I think. I hope, anyway.'

A wave of worry passes across her face and her eyes wander. Searching for something. Something about her nags at Dennira. This girl who is neither too short nor too tall for a human. She knows about the effects of travel, and in realising this Dennira's very soul darkens. Is she a magus? For her own sake she'd best hope not.

'You expect me to believe you don't know how you got here?'

'I know how I got here, my dad sent me, but I'm having some trouble remembering why. But I've no reason to lie. Who are you? Do you live here? Why are you wearing a blindfold?'

Is the light in her eyes friendly or devious? Sometimes it's hard to tell the difference. It's been a long time since Dennira's had another face around to read expressions from. She lowers her staff just an inch, and steps back one pace.

So, the human doesn't remember. That's her story. She scours the girl's face for any trace of deception but none shows. She's good. Whatever scenes she wants to play out she'll act them well. The human kneels quietly, waiting for a response. Tell her nothing.

'Did you understand what I said? Maybe you don't speak the language well?'

Dennira's jaw aches, her gaze hardening.

'I speak your language perfectly well, which should be obvious given we've already been communicating with no issue. Regrettably. I speak more languages than you could ever comprehend from the pitiful selection your world has to offer.'

'Oh uh… sorry I didn't mean to offend you. It's just… you're so quiet and you're just staring. At least I think you are. I thought you hadn't heard or-'

'I'm standing a few feet away. I can hear everything down to your fluttering heart and your shivering fear. What are you doing on my shores?'

'Sorry, I wish I could answer your question. I just need a bit of time…wait…' her eyes widen and her face spreads into a smile. Who would smile in this situation, what's wrong with this girl? 'You can hear my fear? What does it sound like? How can you do that?' She shuffles forward an inch or two on her knees, looking up at Dennira with… excitement? She's excited to be here? How clueless can you get? Dennira pushes her staff into the sand with a hard crunch and the girl flinches. Dennira considers her. Scrutinises her. Doubting her own doubt. Could she be telling the truth?

Humans don't believe the truth even when you tell it to them in absolute candor. Why should she believe this girl's words? She must want something. So far she's shown no hostility, only chronic lack of focus and

21

inappropriate reactions. She doesn't act like an infiltrator. Then again, why would an infiltrator act like one? It would give them away.

She reads the human's soul again, and is unused to the noise of it with being so out of practice. It would be easier without the blindfold, but she hasn't used her power in thirty years and isn't about to go back on that for this intruder. Who's fault is that if not theirs, though?

She reads young, but not as young as Dennira would expect. There's a kindness about her, a strength, but nothing malicious. She's covering it well if it exists within her. She's a pretty girl. It doesn't escape Dennira's notice. She clearly looks after her body, even if she's still a little awkward in its casing. When she grows into herself she will be graceful. Her features give her a somewhat regal look without bordering into arrogant, and her warm, copper skin is rich in colour and smooth. Of course if they were going to send anyone, they'd send someone who leaves a good first impression.

'Is my fear talking to you? What's it saying? Is it something I can learn to do?'

Dennira scoffs. 'You don't have the capacity to learn these things. You're not of a strong enough spirit. Is that what you've come for? The secrets to the pathmaster's power? Our magic is not for you humans to practice.'

The girl blinks in a startled way. 'You… you're a pathmaster? Woah! Are there more of you here? I grew up with stories about you and your kind, I always wanted to meet-'

'Enough.' Dennira's shoulders shake. Her stomach rolls. The girl shuffles back a little more as anger emanates through the sand.

'Sorry, what did I say?'

'You dare intrude on my home after what your kind did and sit there and question me? Ignoring my inquiries, feigning forgetfulness, and having the temerity to speak of my kin? You might as well spit on their spirits yourself.'

'I really don't remember.' The smile cracks now. She's been using it to hide behind. A shield. 'I know I should be able to, but each time I reach for a memory it just… vanishes. Like it's sucked into a vacuum and I've no idea why. I wish I knew. I know everything is there in my head, just under the surface I just can't… my head hurts. It's kind of blurred like cloudy water. Please, can you help?'

'Why would I help you? Or any of your kind given what you did? Go back the way you came or find another way out of here.'

'I don't know the way I came!' Panic laces her words. It's the least composed she's been. A spark of sympathy tries to rise in Dennira, but it's caught in the crossfire of her indignation.

'That's not my problem. Figure it out and get out of here. It's no longer my job to help your kind. You're not my concern.' She turns to storm away but something stops her. Something makes her half-turn back. 'But do not enter the water. Disturbing it could cost you your life, like so many other things around here. You're lucky you didn't land in it else you'd likely be dead already and saved me a job. Don't touch it, don't listen to it, and don't follow the shadows with your eyes. Other than that, you're on your own.'

Lifting her staff out of the sand she strides away, ignoring the desperate spluttering of the human.

As easily as she can choose to hear everything, she can also choose to hear nothing. Not the fear in the girl's words, or the loneliness. Not the panic or the confusion. Not Dennira's problem. Never mind that the symptoms the girl mentioned ring some distant warning bell. Never mind that she's clearly becoming scared. The only sound Dennira hears through the roar of her own annoyance is her hooves making crisp imprints in the grains beneath her. If the girl is still on the island by the end of her lantern rounds then she'll remove her herself. What's one more soul on the kill pile?

That distant warning bell tolls in Dennira's mind as it knits something together. Don't follow the shadows with your eyes. Souls. "I don't remember". Dennira doesn't stop walking, but her gut sinks and compresses into itself. The girl's eyes. They'd been… shining. Shining and silver at the centre of their natural earthen brown.

Humans come in all sorts of shades, just like her own kin. Life is always diverse. But in all her time of being a pathmaster, she's never seen copper skin and eyes with a silver glow. When human souls land here because their physical body is nearing its end, their eyes remain normal. Despite her blocking the way for all souls, sometimes some manage to slip through. Unfortunately for them.

The more Dennira thinks on it, the more she realises that the only time she's ever seen that dull shine in the eyes of humans is when they're here by proxy. Not truly detached from their earthly bodies but forcing their souls onto another plain with magic while their fleshy shells wait at home, which is rare. A dangerous and reckless magic. Hard to control well, and it requires a second magus to maintain the connection while the traveller wanders. It wasn't silver the last time she saw that glow, though. It was a dark red.

The girl is here on a tether. Sent by someone else, her dad she said. What kind of parent sends their daughter to another plain? This is some other kind of magic. Not the magic that was used in the war. War, no, not a war. The massacre. That isn't possible.

Everyone who knows how to make a soul tether should be dead, unless they've re-learned the magic. Dennira should know. She killed most of them herself.

CHAPTER 4

Strange and Beautiful Creature

The midnight blue cloak of the creature sweeps the sand as she strides away, and Kyra battles to stay calm. Somehow she's managed to cause offence, or at least anger. Though, come to think of it, the anger seemed to be there from the start. Maybe even more than that. It feels like hate. This is nothing new to Kyra and her father. They've fought against the prejudice of the other magi for years, and will keep on fighting it. Her mind stirs. Images clot and bleed to try and knit themselves together. Hopefully she'll remember something soon, travelling doesn't normally muddle her this much, but for now she has to put things right.

'Wait!' She scrambles to her feet, shivering as the shoreline swoops up the beach to get a little too close for comfort. She's never run on sand before, but she's glad the beach is quite short. Grass feels more firm underfoot. The creature walks with impossible grace for her extra height and has the gait of a giant. If she's the only company Kyra has until she figures things out, then she has to fix their disastrous first encounter. 'Excuse me, sorry, please wait. I didn't mean to cause offence, I'm just a bit rattled. I'm Kyra. What's your name? And how can you see where you're going?'

By the time the questions are out Kyra has drawn alongside the pathmaster, but not too close. She knows she's asking too many, but can't help it. It's too interesting a situation to hold them back. The silver staff glints in the strange light of the sky that doesn't have a sun, and the small bell tinkles as they walk. 'I like the sound of your bell. It's very calming. And I've never seen blue fire before, is it different to regular fire?' No response. Not so much as a flicker of facial expression. Maybe she is made of porcelain, after all?

The entrance to a copse of trees looms before them, clearly overgrown and somewhat unkempt. 'Is this where you live? It looks… cosy. Back home we live in an old terraced house, but my dad made the loft into a special space for us to practice our magic.' Stride, swish, stride, swish. The only sounds coming from the pathmaster. Kyra might as well not be here at all.

In a wild leap of imagination her brain presents the possibility that she's been turned invisible, but she pushes it away. 'I just had a few questions about some of the things you said. It sounds like I've done something wrong and I just want to know what. You said "your kind aren't welcome", did you mean humans?' A blast of wind rustles through the foliage as they pass through the entrance to the little forest.

For a few moments Kyra thinks it beautiful, like some kind of enchanted forest. Maybe she's ended up in the fairy realm or something. Unfamiliar shapes hide in the overgrown impressions of nature to create shadows and unusual constructions. Slowing a little, unable to keep the creature's effortless pace, Kyra catches her breath and looks closer. Buildings? Wrapped in vines and choked by nature. Piles of rough materials are scattered about. There are so many. What did they used to be?

'What is this place? It looks like it used to have some buildings here. Maybe a market or something?'

Stride, swish, stride, swish. Further away she walks. Talkative as stone. Comforting as a tomb. Kyra balls her hands into fists. Tension seeps into her shoulders. She's always been taught that ignorance is rude. She's been nothing but apologetic since arriving, but so far this pathmaster wasn't living up to the stories whatsoever. They're meant to be helpful and caring. Wise and comforting. Building bridges between worlds for souls to pass through. Those details, at least, she does remember. Something rises in her and bursts out before she can stop it.

'Don't pathmasters have any manners? Or do you all wear ignorance like arrogance?' The creature stops. Kyra's skin raises in goosebumps against the sensation of her target bristling with disdain. Her words echo like the mistake they are, carving deep grooves into the inside of her lungs.

With a swoosh the pathmaster whips around, thumping her staff against the overgrown ground. The black strip of the blindfold bores into Kyra as the creature's top lip curls into a snarl. She'd likely shrivel under a ferocious gaze without the blindfold's obscuring protection. Silence crackles between them for uncounted seconds, and then her stomach drops into her legs as the pathmaster starts towards her.

'My arrogance? The insolence of humans knows no bounds it seems. The manners of my kin meant nothing to you in the past and you do not deserve them in the present, nor will you ever deserve them again. I owe you nothing. Less than nothing. If anything I owe you death or worse.'

Kyra backs away, but her aggressor keeps on coming. Stride after hooved stride. Staff shining dangerously as the fire it houses flares brighter every second. This is a mistake, she's gone too far, but can't undo her words now. Any attempt to apologise twists into a frightened squeak or pours out of her in beads of sweat.

'Whoever sent your soul here, you'd better hope they recall you soon. Breaking your tether would be as easy to me as snipping a thread. I would barely have to think about it or even look in your direction to do it. Mention my kin again and I will cut your cord from this and all plains, and you'll float like the speck of nothing you deserve to be for what your previous generations did to me and mine.'

Whack. Kyra's back meets the trunk of a twisting tree. There's nowhere to go. No way to get out. Still the pathmaster comes, her face etched with lines of hate. She bends forward, bringing her bloodless face so close to Kyra she can smell the scent of the earth and tang of herbs. Something ripples in the back of Kyra's mind. Something big and that carries enormous weight. If it's her memories rising from the depths of her brain fog then she'd very much like them to hurry up about it.

'I wished to live the rest of my life without seeing another human, but still you come to my shores. Never satisfied with what you've already taken. Bringing forth selfish requests. Why must you continue to make me dispose of you? That was never my desire. It goes against everything me and mine ever worked for and yet you forced our hand and this,' she gestures around to the wild space they stand in, 'is the result.

'I don't care what request you come bearing, the moment your memory returns I expect you to remove your poisonous presence from my home, and if you so much as dare look back I will ensure the last thing you see is flame. Am I clear?' With excruciating and desperately reserved movements the staff is brought forward and Kyra flinches automatically.

Her heart hammers against the inside of her ribcage. This is it. She's going to be burned alive right here on this spot. With a hollow knock the staff hits the tree trunk and the little bell calls out in its merry dance. The roots and limbs of the flora surrounding the tree wriggle to life and wind themselves around Kyra. They pull tight around her waist and lower extremities.

'Wait, what are you doing? Please stop I-'

'I said: Am I clear?' The words hiss through gritted teeth. Kyra can only manage a nervous nod. 'This tree will bind you long enough for me to get some distance from your incessant questioning. Use the time well to reclaim your memory and then get yourself off my island, whatever it takes.' One step back, then another, and the creature retreats. Yet as Kyra watches her walk away a rush of strength, or maybe defiance, pushes its way upward and out.

'May I ask your name?' The pathmaster stops again, but doesn't ooze anger this time. 'If I'm to be left here alone I'd at least like to know your name so that I can remember you. Or if not yours the name of someone else on this island who might be of help.'

She keeps her tone respectful and light, but serious and solemn. Will she even be able to hear the answer over the whizz of her blood as her heart shoots it around her body? The creature sighs. It's deep and sad, which only leads to more questions in Kyra's mind.

'My name is Dennira. Mine is the only name you need to know, as I'm the last remaining inhabitant on these shores. There is no one else here to assist you. Please do as I ask. I've not the strength to ask again.' And with that she takes her sadness and vanishes into the trees before Kyra can even ask what she means. Questions have done her no good so far, after all.

What does she mean? There are so many things she said that stir strong feelings in Kyra. Every word she recalls from Dennira triggers something deep within. Something she hopes will surface soon, but it feels as though something is blocking the way. A barrier withholding access to her own mind. She can't remember anything recent now. Only things from long ago or apparently things that are new. Dennira. A strange and beautiful name. A strange and beautiful creature.

What now? The roots won't part by Kyra's will, not that she expects them to. She's trapped and has no idea for how long. Tied to a tree on an island with one very grouchy inhabitant and a gap where a chunk of her memory should be. The rest in danger of being slurped up by whatever fog of confusion she can't shake. She has to figure something out, anything. She has to fix this.

CHAPTER 5

Nothing but a Husk

A storm broils in Dennira as she pulls out of the forest on to the path back up towards the cliffs. A flurry of utter weariness that buzzes with adrenaline and the scathing heat of disbelief. Arriving somewhere by tether could have an effect on memory in a temporary way, that is true enough. To claim to have forgotten the whole history of the actions of her people, though? While still somehow recalling childhood stories of pathmasters? No, it must be a lie. Some kind of ploy or ironic jibe.

The girl, Kyra she said her name was, can't be serious. Practically skipping along the beach next to her asking innocent and inquisitive questions. Pretending to have grown up on awe-inspiring stories. The only stories of her kind left in the human world were damning and outrageously tainted.

She lights lanterns as she goes, all of them concerned for her and asking what happened. In gentle apology she tells them not worry and that everything will be fine. She'll continue to protect them no matter the cost to herself. As she moves back into range of the lantern that sits atop the cliffs the bell on her staff chimes inquisitively.

'I've no idea why she's here, why would I know that?'

Another chorus of jingling replies. 'I didn't let her stay, I just didn't clip her tether. She'll probably fade in time if she doesn't leave soon.' Rounding the corner to the cliff's plateau she longs for nothing more than lying in the comfort of her cave until tomorrow, and hopes that when she re-emerges the human is gone. 'I don't know how she did it. They shouldn't be able to get here, all the traditional gates are gone. The magic used to send her… it's too similar to the magic from back then.' A note or two jingles.

'Yeah, similar. Not the same. Her eyes were silver, not red.'

Dennira looks back down at the treetops that cover the old settlement in the distance. A pang of guilt creases her middle but she shakes it off.

'It's not my concern. Her memory loss does seem severe, but that could be to do with the magic.'

The sea and sky are calm and quiet. Perhaps too quiet. But everything sounds quiet in the face of her boiling blood. The small bell chides her.

'I will be calm soon, it's just a shock is all. It's been years since I had to deal with one. Though it's the first one who has washed up on the shore like that. If she landed in the water she should be dead. That or she has the luck of the five moons on her side. Maybe they're planning to come back. Maybe they're coming back to kill me, to kill the last of us. I can't do it again, Annika, I can't. Once was enough.'

The blue flame takes on its lightest shade and snakes around Dennira's arm. It moves up over her shoulder and caresses her cheek, cupping it in its warmth. The fear and tension fade. Receding back down into the realms of

Dennira's control. 'Why can't we just be left in peace? Her even being here will be like a beacon. The longer she stays the more unwanted company will descend on our home.' The bell makes a suggestion, and a good one at that.

'Alright, I'll go to the Ingress. It's as good a place as any to hide until that thing leaves.'

It would take a newcomer years to learn all the secret and winding paths of the island. The great, jagged clod of rock that builds the back end is more than just solid wall-to-wall stone. Spaces are hidden away in pockets all throughout its aimless structure, forged over centuries by Dennira and her kin.

The Ingress is the closest thing to pass for sacred to the pathmasters, aside from the soul bridges themselves. Dennira makes light work of the dangerous path hidden among the jutting surface of the eastern cliffs. Her agility is well-honed and built in to her nature. Not even a pebble is uprooted from its resting place as she negotiates her way down with the grace of a dancer on pointe. It would be easy to pass the opening, just like it's easy to pass by all the island's secrets until you know about their existence.

The opening folds out into a rocky tunnel that curves around and down on a slight incline. It opens out into a rough-cut circular space paved with rich green grass and white flowers that grow nowhere else on the island. They idle in small groups next to the mist-flecked pool that's fed by a curtain of water as it pours out from the rock higher up. Dennira smiles as she breathes in the air of the fresh spring.

Sitting at the pond-side, legs curled up next to her,

she lights the silver lanterns and sits and waits for them to gather.

Small blue spheres, like fireflies, rise from the white flowers and orbit the space freely. They chime among themselves, sometimes playing with the bell or the flame on Dennira's staff as it stands propped against a nearby wall. Here is the only place she can be surrounded by her people.

They sing to her the way they used to sing in the settlement when it bustled with life, sounds and smells. Her guards all fall away, shed layer by layer with each line of song that wraps around her, letting her know she's valued and important to someone, anyone.

She swirls the water gently with her fingers. A single ring on her middle finger connects to a bracelet by a delicate chain. A gift from Annika on the day they became bonded. She tries to remember the good if she has to remember at all. But the chaos always looms underneath. A sticky heat threatening to crack the facade of her efforts to keep it buried. Shining through under the surface like lava waiting to break free and burn everything inside her to leave nothing but a husk. She's been that husk before, and doesn't want to go back.

How can you know, though? How can you know you're still you without someone else there to confirm it? The flicker of a flame isn't the same as the contact of a hand. Or the skin of another. Eventually the former replaces the latter. Things fade out of memory. The alternative becoming the thing it imitates.

The song of the spheres pushes away all the sadness for Dennira. For a while she sings with them, joining her voice to theirs, and for a moment she's not alone.

For a moment she's surrounded by her people. But only a moment. She can't suspend disbelief enough to lose herself in her wishful thinking completely. Being alone makes you practical. Too practical for delusions, anyway.

Speaking of being practical, she hasn't even finished her tasks for the day. She promised Jennir she'll harvest the crystal herbs soon. If she leaves it too long they will gradually lose their medicinal qualities. There is only one place on the island where they grow, and Dennira often puts off visiting it until the last possible moment.

The Nethercove. Another island secret like the Ingress. The place holds too many memories. The happiest ones are sometimes the most painful to relive. The most stark reminder of what's been snatched from her grasping hands.

She'll go, but later when she's gathered herself a bit. The chiming notes of her kins' song is already soothing and calming her. Easing away all the tremors of the acidic emotions that have been stirred up in her on this day.

Dennira leans back, about to lie on the grass, when the song changes. The notes morph to their minor cousins, dripping with caution and warning. A haunting drone that urges her to action.

'Hide yourselves, and stay safe.'

They do as they're bid, the silence ringing louder in the cavern than the songs ever did. A chilling wind swirls in the circular space and Dennira's heart skips. If the wind is warning her down here, in one of the few places it shouldn't be able to venture, then something's wrong. The next gust brings a sample of an acrid smell and she covers her nose with the sleeve of her robe.

The human is one thing, but this new visitor Kyra's presence has attracted is entirely another.

CHAPTER 6

Moths Don't Talk

The silence presses in around Kyra as a smothering shawl. Well, not true silence, but one filled with noises that only conjure eerie feelings. The rustling of the foliage, the distant breathing of the dangerous sea. The strange chirps and calls of who knows what kind of insects and creepy crawlies. Her arms and legs ache from trying to free herself from Dennira's obedient tree, and in a huff Kyra slumps in her bonds and lets out a sharp sigh.

She has no idea what to make of Dennira. Weariness starts to seep into her joints as her energy and adrenaline subside. What a day. Or maybe it's night. It's eternal twilight in this place. The stony expressions of the pathmaster warp from empty to brimming with disgust over and over, and yet Kyra can't deny the curious urge to see what lies beneath her blindfold. What could have happened to make her so bitter? She's never been more curious about another living being, and for Kyra that's saying something.

'How is tying me to a tree going to be of any use or help me get home quicker?' she asks the empty clearing. 'And what's her problem? She was so hostile and I haven't done anything wrong, have I?' Thinking back Kyra had definitely put her foot in her mouth once or twice, though that's nothing new.

Aside from that she's been polite and respectful, over-curious of course but that's as certain as the sun rising each morning. Here that means it's not very sure at all, she supposes. Think before you ask, that's what her dad always tried to instill in her, but it rarely worked.

With nothing else to do she takes the time to think now. Her small selection of magus abilities were left behind with her body on the human plain. You can't take them with you when you travel, not that any of her skills could have helped her in this situation. Though perhaps if she'd paid more attention when her dad tried to explain the basics of botanical magic she could have at least persuaded the tree to loosen its grip a little. Probably not, actually. You have to be extremely respectful and polite to plants and trees to get them to fulfill requests, and Kyra is already sitting on this one without permission. Would have been worth a try, though.

She looks around, slowing her mind down and really inspecting her surroundings. Work with what you know. Dennira had pushed her right across what could be a village square. A crumbling well or fountain sits in the middle, and Kyra deflects the idea that some weird creature is crouching just inside its lip. Waiting for its chance to gobble up a seventeen-year-old human girl.

There are more buildings than she initially noticed. They're all of a similar size. All in different stages of disrepair. There's no pattern to their placement, just small groups huddled together. The more she searches them out, the more she finds. Huts is the most suitable word she can attach to the structures. Huts… homes?

A rush of pins and needles cover her body top to bottom before vanishing. Are the huts destroyed homes? Did this used to be a settlement? Dennira's voice returns to her thoughts as though to confirm her unasked question. *"Mine is the only name you need to know, as I'm the last remaining inhabitant on these shores."*

The last one? Doesn't that suggest there were others? If she's the only one left then where did they go? *"Mention my kin again and I will cut your cord from this and all plains and you'll float like the speck of nothing you deserve to be for what your previous generations did to me and mine."*

She lives here alone? Completely alone with no company at all? Kyra is already working with all her energy to stem her own panic and she's barely been alone for half an hour. How does Dennira do it day after day? The quiet. The ever-expanding space around a single body. Sentient things need sentient company. To fill the space around them and diffuse the widening maw of silence.

Kyra's chest aches for Dennira as she wonders how long this ruined island has been the place she and she alone has called home. Living with nothing but the hush of the sea and the memories of what used to be.

'What did we do? Humans can't have done this.' Her mind whirs, dancing around admitting it. Dennira's anger, her hostility and disdain towards Kyra for no reason, could it be warranted? If they did this, destroyed this place… no, no there was no way.
She would have been told about it. Her dad would have told her.

A blinding flash shines behind her eyes as she tries

to access her memories. Nothing. Nothing to grasp, nothing to pull forward, just white slowly being poisoned by black ink. It starts at the edges and plumes in. It's gone as abruptly as it began. Why can't she remember anything? Or rather, why is she remembering less and less. As though simply reaching for a memory is enough to make it disappear.

The only person she can think of other than herself is her dad, but he's out of reach. She just has the word 'dad' and a blurry image. That's the last pull pin in her control over her panic, and once pulled it begins to bubble and broil and spill out into her body. She's losing her memories. All of them.

As if acting as a calming distraction, the largest moth Kyra has ever seen bobs towards her almost head-on. It sways and floats. A leaf lost on a gentle wind current. Its wings curl slightly at the edges with each flap. Flaps she can hear due to the size of the insect.

They're onyx black with shimmering veins of blue painting patterns of criss-crossed branches across their surface. And its eyes. Its eyes are bright blue. She tracks it as it flutters towards her, and her panic recedes with each wing-beat. Insects aren't something to be feared. They're part of the world just like anything else. Everything has the right to live its allotted time. These lessons were all taught to her by someone important. But who? Who said the words.

A smile spreads across her face as the huge moth lands on her forearm. There's a delicate weight to it. Its long legs fidget on the deep green fabric of her sleeve.

'Hello there. You're quite a big fellow, aren't you? Perhaps your name is Absolem. Are you from

Wonderland? Maybe that's where I am. It could be for all I know.' Unsurprisingly the moth doesn't respond. 'You're very pretty.' A small batting of the wings could well be a thank you. Someone used to read that book to her when she was young. Someone important. But who? Who read the book? 'I don't suppose you can free me?' That single wing-beat could well be a no. 'I didn't think so. I wonder when she'll set me free?'

'Kyra.'

She swallows her gasp, trying not to startle the moth. Then she stares at the insect itself. Is that where it came from? You're going to have to get a hold of yourself, Kyra, moths don't talk. Even though today you spoke with a woman who appears to be half-human, half-deer.

'Kyra.' It comes again. A slimey and thick whisper from somewhere behind... behind what? It moves. Snaking through the air. The moth takes flight and departs for the broken canopy of trees. Off into the sky. She's alone again. She waits for the third whisper of her name.

'Who said that?' The instant the words leave her mouth a blanket of dread wraps around her. Another mistake. She's making a lot of those today. Why on Earth would answering to a disembodied voice on an unfamiliar island when tied to a tree be a good idea? After a few seconds of silence her worry is confirmed. It asked and she answered. That soft, malicious laugh seething through the ruined settlement isn't real. Nope. Not real. Denial or not, the smoke comes.

The first tendril creeps over the lip of the well and every muscle in Kyra's body goes rigid. Is there something hiding in there after all? Has she disturbed it?

Then it starts to flood in from her left, and her right. It's everywhere and nowhere all at once.

'Come with me, Kyra.'

The voice turns her stomach but its words turn her mind. Rolling it like a pickle in a jar, kneading it like bread dough. A headache blooms and she clamps her mouth closed, refusing to answer the beckoning again. A shadow glides between two trees across the square. It's so slow she almost misses it, picking it up in the corner of her vision and not quite seeing it. Does that make it better or worse? She doesn't know. It comes again, rising to look over at her through a cracked window frame on the opposite side to where she saw it the first time. Is it moving quickly, or is there more than one?

The questions don't help. If only she could mute her mind, but then again if she did that there would be more room for her fear to grow. Bile bubbles in her stomach. Her lungs fail to pick just one working rhythm. Stinging flourishes in her eyes from being so wide for so long. If she shouts Dennira, the only available inhabitant of the island, will she come? Kyra knows the answer, and curses the quiet tears that confirm it.

CHAPTER 7

An Otherworldly Lighthouse

Dennira bounds across the island's familiar landscape. She doesn't even need to think about her footing, which is just as well since her mind is calculating other things. They're getting bold, these creatures. The draw of a human soul after all this time is too great for them to remember her warnings. Sometimes they bore of what the sea has to offer and come out to claim greater prizes.

When the island was full of her kin, the denizens of the sea rarely dared set foot out of the shallow water lest they face a sound beating from the pathmasters. After what happened, though, they've learned that there's only Dennira here to protect the place. However, there are no longer as many human souls on offer for them to try and snatch.

As she departs the jagged path of the cliffs she skids to a stop on the dirt track leading into the main forest. Her sensitive nose objects to the smell of burning wood, and right on cue she spots wisps of black smoke slinking through the trees. A covet eel? A malicious one, too. It must be coming for the girl. It's her own fault. If she wants to walk around on a soul tether then she has to face the risks.

Dennira's bell tinkles and she scoffs.

'I know it was me who tied her to the tree, but she just wouldn't stop following me. And the questions, you've never heard so many.' She starts forward into the murky smoke, keeping her voice low and listening to signs that the eel might be close by. Even the volume of the bell seems lower. 'I know I said she wasn't my concern. I'm not doing this for her, I'm doing it to protect our home. Don't forget this creature could have come here to try and take the spirits from the lanterns, too.' The bell chides her and she shakes her head from side to side with a sigh. 'Let me focus.'

Crouching at the base of a tree, Dennira listens and thinks. She has the advantage, knowing that the eel is likely headed for the girl and knowing that the girl can't move. She slaps away the distant echo of guilt and tells herself it isn't warranted. The eel itself is somewhat vulnerable on land, so it sends out its smoke. A common trait of the sea creatures of this plain.

First a clear variant to confuse the victim and feed whispers or visions to spook and scare so it can better smell them. Their eyesight is poor aside from being able to see the astral glow of souls, which if you want an otherworldly lighthouse a soul will do just fine. Then comes the black smoke, full of haunting visions and visual tricks. And while the victim deals with that, sending out beacons of adrenaline to mark their location, the eel slithers ashore, dragging itself on lizard-like legs. Then before you know it you're in its jaws.

The human plain has eels, but not like this one. Not ones that can walk and attack with neurological tricks. Or ones that are the size of a large crocodile. Alright Dennira, think.

'I'd better check if she's even still alive first.' The bell perks up. 'Yes, I know she told me her name. Are you really going to try and give away my position on the basis of pleasantries?' The bell holds still. 'Fine, let's check if Kyra is still alive.' The blue flame brightens in approval.

Dennira lies her staff on the ground and places both hands over it. Her fingers pass into the earth up to the first knuckle and she connects with the underground roots. 'Find the human, please' she asks them. Her voice full of respect. They acquiesce and her vision is drawn through them as they show her the world through their senses.

Along the way she chooses trees to climb for a better view, but it takes a few tries to find one that overlooks the village square well enough to see what's happening. The smoke is everywhere, churning like waves far out to sea, but it only comes to waist height. Even if it didn't, the roots can see through it easily.

There's no sign of the eel yet, but nor is there any sign of Kyra's consciousness. Trying to discern the world through smudged greys, whites and shadows takes a lot of practice, but there are things that also stand out like spotlights. Creatures and living things all have their shades. Humans, though? They sear the black and white landscape with their blue glow... if they're conscious.

Dennira knows where she left her, and strains her vision to find the correct tree. Kyra is slumped in her bonds, breathing erratically and twitching. The eel is already showing her visions. Soon it will haul itself out of the sea and come to claim her. If Dennira releases Kyra's bonds she'll fall to the ground with no way to catch herself. She pulls her vision out of the tree and darts through the underground network of life, moving so fast her physical body feels the tip of the world's axis.

She checks the closest shore, knowing that these things always take the shortest route to their prey. If anything, Kyra's lucky its only an eel. They aren't so tough to deal with.

A shadow meanders idly in the shallows, waiting for the right time to go in for the kill. There isn't much time. She snaps back into her physical body, thanking the roots for their assistance.

Dennira sits back on her haunches and considers. If the eel takes the girl then her problem is solved. No humans on her island and the wretched creature will be sated for years on one soul alone. However, the soul will give it more power and help it to grow. It may even call some of its larger, more dangerous friends to these waters under the promise of a soul buffet. Not much chance of that but still. It could come back itself in future wanting more of that power, and the only place it will find it here is in Dennira or in the lanterns. She won't put what's left of her kin at risk. Not when she can save the girl and then Kyra can go home when she remembers how. Correction, save the island, not save the girl. Her days of helping humans are over, this is merely a conflict of interests.

She lingers too long again on the idea of just letting the eel have its way. But the unknown problems down the line are too much of a wild card to let it happen. She doesn't want the covet eel spreading the word about the island, nor does she want to be endlessly circled by a twisting shoal of creatures while they wait for the next potential meal to wash up on the beach. They might be slow and near-useless on land, but in the sea? You'd find yourself dead without the eels ever making so much as a ripple.

The bell trills urgently as she lifts herself from the ground.

'No, I won't let it eat her. Why are you so concerned?' A chorus of chimes rings a little too loudly. 'It's not our job to look after them anymore, Annika. They made sure of that back then.' She sighs heavily, drawing her fingers across her forehead at the same time. 'Yes, yes I'm going. And yes I'll free her, but I'm not doing it for her. I'm doing it to avoid more trouble in the future.'

The bell's response is full of sarcasm and Dennira chuckles inwardly. Even in this form, a shade of the wonderful person she'd been in life, Annika still gives her a hard time and acts like a true pathmaster should. Now isn't the time to remember how much she misses her, though. Now is the time to do something she hasn't done for just over thirty years. She has to help a human soul.

CHAPTER 8

Harsh Words but Kind Actions

Screams echo and howl in Kyra's mind. They spark through her nervous system in bolts of captured lightning, but she can't move her body to discharge the pressure. Visions storm in great, disturbing clouds. She disintegrates and reassembles, only to fragment again as she tries to touch her face. Her hand melts off of her skeleton, then reforms itself just as easily. The scenery flickers wildly. The island, her home, the deep sea, the twisted undergrowth of a cold forest. Nausea rises and recedes again and again.

She stands before a mirror and watches her soul peel away from her body. It wanders through the glass and over a bridge with shining, ornate carvings on the transparent wooden slats. Shouting for it not to go, Kyra finds that her mouth has gone and luminous blue blood pools at her feet. Dennira strides towards her from the dark, her face furrowed with hate, and uses her staff to break a tether that materialises between Kyra and the mirror. She's cut from her soul as it wanders away along that lonely bridge, and she falls backward into an abyss that wraps its arms around her. An old friend.

She doesn't fight it. She just falls. Fades. Forgets. Then with a jolt she opens her eyes, and a thick scent washes over her. Where is she? The ceiling above her is carved from stone, far too smooth to be a natural space. Think about what you know. It will keep you calm. Yet Kyra finds that she knows nothing, and fights to stop the tears from spilling over her already blurry eyes.

Unfamiliar noises wheedle their way into her ears. A coarse grinding and rustle of what sounds like dried leaves. The tinkle of a bell at random intervals and whispers in a language she can't comprehend. The words entwine with each other like fine silk and twist into patterns in her mind. Her body is dead weight, too heavy to lift any one part. Instead she turns her neck, dragging herself off of the cushion of her hair and flinching in pain as she looks around.

Dennira is kneeling in the corner by a small hearth that burns with a dancing flame. Her blue cloak pools around her as she works, and Kyra is fascinated. Each gesture seems to mean more than its actions. She works with a pestle of smooth grey stone next to a small incense lantern. Her every movement is precise as she manifests stoppered bottles and chooses ingredients one by one. Inspecting each item before adding it to the mix and stirring with her delicate wrists that make short work of turning the plants to paste.

Images trickle in. Images of seeing strange shapes dash about in a thick black fog. Has Dennira chosen to help her after all? Brought her back here… wherever here is.

Her throat has been replaced with sandpaper, but she manages to force her words over it. They sound rough and croaky, but form what she intended to say. At least she hopes so.

'Thank you.'

Dennira's movements slow but she doesn't look up. 'I didn't do it for you.' There's no malice in her words this time, just neutral calm. Matter-of-fact statements. Another waft from the incense clears Kyra's mind a fraction more. The faint recognition of lavender is mixed in with the other notes of the perfume that she's never encountered before.

'What happened, and where are we?'

'I wondered when the questions would resume.'

'Sorry.' Kyra sighed. 'I just don't remember what happened.'

'A creature tried to turn you into its prey.'

They come again. The images of the strange shape lurking. Circling. Being trapped and unable to free herself. Yet they're already fading.

'Why was I tied up?'

Dennira does look at her now. Slowly raising her head to lock eyes with Kyra, if her eyes had been visible. Maybe she can see through that blindfold somehow after all.

'You don't remember?' The lightest impression of concern creases her brow.

'No, just that I couldn't move after the smoke came. I couldn't get away even after I saw the thing moving toward me. The memory is already vanishing like the others.'

Kyra makes the smallest effort to move her body, longing to sit up, and the world tilts violently on an axis it shouldn't have.

'Don't try and sit up. You're still tainted by the smoke. It will take time for the incense to remove it.'

'Why can't I remember anything? Everytime I try, the thing I want to remember disappears.' Palpitations beat a staggered rhythm on the drums of panic. Calling to it and drawing it up from deep within. The void where her memory should be, where her past should be, is empty and there's no way to ground her mind. She can't draw on what she knows because the answer is nothing. Only her own name, the name of the creature grinding leaves, and the images of the faceless shape that loomed forward in the gloom while she was trapped.

She draws in too many short breaths too quickly and chokes on the incense that's meant to help her. Each cough echoes in her every nerve. Pins and needles bloom as fireworks in different places and she can't lie there anymore. Kyra forces herself upright. Dennira's objections are lost in a flash so bright that Kyra is blinded and knocked sideways.

Darkness swirls with inky colours for a while. Sounds melt in the distance. Cool hands that smell of the earth rest against her forehead and her mind lets in the visitor who knocks before entering. Then something starts to come away. Dragged like a thorny net across the surface of her brain. A stubborn stain resistant to anything but scouring. A warmth comes forward and peels it away, its barbs catching here and there in its reluctance to detach.

Whispers echo, they say to be calm and hold still, and Kyra listens. She sinks into the ground as the rigidity of fear dissolves. With a final, sticky tug and damp slurping sound in her ear the feeling is gone from her mind. A wave of coldness swoops in to drape over her. Her mind has never been so quiet. She rises back into her body to find herself on the floor while the cool stone warms slightly under her feverish body. Dennira, who is kneeling next to her, stands in an elegant motion and carries something away in one hand. With a sweeping gesture she summons a jar and places something in it. Something that writhes and wriggles in a way that sends shivers through Kyra's spine.

'What... what is that?' Of course the first thing out of her mouth is a question.

'It's a memoracle. You must have picked it up from the sea. It burrows into the mind and consumes memories.'

A mix of a large slug and a weird crab is the only way Kyra can describe it. Beady black eyes on fleshy sticks, too many legs, a long, squishy body, but its movements are far faster than any slug. It shoots around the jar in angry defeat.

'You pulled that out of my head? But I didn't enter the sea.' The thought coats Kyra in a crust of dirt and she bolts upright, staring at the bizarre creature, and recoils at the image of it being anywhere inside her. Then she recalls her wet jean leg. That small contact with the water was all it took for something to catch hold and crawl up her body? The room swings on a pendulum and she has to steady herself.

'Yes. They're so rare I didn't consider you might have been targeted by one. I'll extract your memories from it and return them to you.'

'You can do that?'

'It wouldn't do to leave your mind vacant. It would only serve as a vessel for something else to make a home of it.'

Kyra watches with interest and Dennira puts a hand either side of the jar while a soft white glow blooms from her palms. The angry creature starts to still and a glittering fog siphons out of its leech-like mouth. The stopper of the vial lifts just enough for what Kyra assumes are her stolen memories to gather in a twirling ball that grows a little every few seconds.

The more Dennira draws out of it, the thinner the memoracle becomes. It looks spent and exhausted when she's done. Thin like a treacle-black worm instead of fat on precious pilfered experiences. The vial re-stoppers the creature's prison and Dennira holds the memories in one hand, storing the memoracle safely away with the other.

'Woah.' Kyra can't help but gawp. Dennira's use of magic is so refined and specific, not clumsy like some of Kyra's own attempts. She's improved a lot in the past few years but as her dad loves to remind her, it takes a long time to become not just a proficient but an efficient magus. Dennira doesn't waste a single scrap of magic at all.

'Close your eyes.'

Kyra does as she's bid and a few seconds later a feeling of warm water fills the same ear the memoracle was pulled from. It whirls through her mind, but doesn't show any signs of settling.

'It will take a little time for your memories to recover completely. They'll need to slot themselves back into their rightful places and knit themselves back together. But after that you shouldn't have any more problems.'

'Thank you. Thank you so much.'

Dennira's shoulders stiffen. 'As I said before, I didn't do any of it for you.'

Kyra flinches, but not from her disgust at the memoracle. Dennira's words have an edge again, and it keens as she continues talking. 'When your memory returns, you'll remember why you're here and how to get home. Perhaps then I can be left in peace.'

She's so hard to read. Stoic and controlled most of the time, skilled at hiding her feelings. Yet she contradicts herself between her words and her actions.

'Whether you did it for me or not, I still want to thank you. It seems you've saved my life twice now if what you say is true.'

'Why would I need to lie about it? Allowing the first creature to claim you would lead to more trouble for this island in the future. Every moment you're here you put the island in greater chances of danger from the many things that feed off of things like you. The second creature prevents you from being able to recall how to leave. That's all there is to it.'

'I see. I'm sorry to have troubled you, then.' Kyra can't help the defiant tone that sneaks in, but Dennira doesn't react to it. She doesn't react at all until Kyra tries to stand.

'You should rest longer and let the incense do its work. It won't take long. You can either stay where you are or get back on the bed, I don't care which you choose.'

Then she went back to grinding things in her mortar. Her face unmarked by any of the feelings that may or may not be bubbling under the surface. Something caught in Kyra's mind. The bed. Dennira had said the bed.

Kyra looks around properly and realisation widens

her eyes. The space is almost cosy. Bare bones, but very clearly a home. A rectangular alcove opens up into the wall of the cave and a soft pad covers its base. There's no blanket, but its definitely a bed. The hearth is in the middle of the space, and tunnels lead off on either wall. A crude table or workbench is carved from the stone near the back of the cave.

This is her home. Dennira brought Kyra into her home to save her. It doesn't match up with the impression Kyra has of the creature so far. Harsh words but kind actions. Hateful expressions but comforting treatments. An uncertainty buzzes around in Kyra's mind. Just what is Dennira and why is she so conflicted?

CHAPTER 9

A Terrible Mistake

With every grind of the mortar and pestle another drop of guilt ripples in the pool of Dennira's core. They fight with the ripples coming from the other side. The ones smeared with rage and outrage and sadness and everything in between. Dennira never thought herself one for hypocrisy, but today it pours out of her in such chaotic waves that it's surprising Kyra can't see it swirling around her like the black smoke of the covet eel. Or maybe she can.

A wave of sympathy for the girl surges forward as Dennira thinks over her own actions so far. It must be confusing. To be met with such hostility and then in the next breath have your life saved by the same aggressor.

How is anyone meant to sort through such an emotional tangle? The part of her that continues to snap at the human is indignant at having one of them in her home, but the part that grinds the herbs for the poultice is reaching. Reaching back through the decades for the natural instinct of the pathmasters to care for humans, or their souls at least. To care for and to guide them.

Kyra sits there now, staring. Perhaps mesmerised by her movements, perhaps brewing a question or trying to stop one from spilling out. The hearth crackles, the leaves grind under her steady rhythm, and the tension grows.

She steals a glance over and meets the girl's shining silver eyes only briefly. Her heart squeezes a little. There's a reason she hasn't been looking at Kyra often. A reason she doesn't want to admit but is so blatant and raw that to acknowledge it could be a dangerous thing. This human reminds her very much of Annika.

The differences are slight. Kyra's warm copper skin tone is much lighter than Annika's. Her nose not quite as broad, and she certainly doesn't yet have the body of a woman. But the resemblance is there and it tugs on Dennira's heart every time she lays eyes on the girl. The human's bold and curious spirit is almost an exact match as well. Kyra is a thief. A thief of Annika, and she's wearing her wrong but also so right. Is this why she can't help but save her? She would have left her. She was going to leave her. Something stopped her and it made her feel weak that this might be the reason why.

A blast of longing smacks against Dennira's heart and she pauses. Fighting the urge to go out and summon Annika's spirit for a few minutes just to feel near to her. Pathmasters bond for life. A bond that will never break and can never be renewed or reassigned.

'What's wrong?' The girl's voice punctures the longing and Dennira calmly resumes her grinding, fighting the rising flush in her cheeks. She's caught off guard. Caught while vulnerable. Something she's not used to.

'It's none of your concern.' The words are sharp, each the strike of a surprised viper, and straight away Dennira winces at herself as Kyra flinches again.

'Alright, look.' Kyra sits straight and embers light her eyes. Dennira can see that her heart rate leaps and bounds as she prepares her words. 'You've made it clear that I'm not welcome here, and that's fine. But there's no way for me to get home until my memory returns. I've done nothing to you, though it sounds like you have something against humans. I'm stuck here now. Despite that, and despite your clear and unquestionable hatred of me… you saved me.'

Dennira's heart rattles now too.

'It's confusing and contradictory and I don't understand why you brought me to your home or are trying to help me after the things you said on the beach. You're giving me whiplash and I've had enough of it. You look upset, so I asked what's wrong. That's what people do, that's the nice thing to do, and in response you practically spit at me. You said you've been alone a long time, but surely not so long that you'd strike out at someone who just wanted to check you're OK?'

It's a question but not quite. Kyra steadies her breathing and glares expectantly. What could Dennira possibly say? She knows she's saying one thing and doing another. Knows she's conflicted and erratic and fighting to figure out her feelings. Is it necessary to snap and snipe at the girl every time she speaks? Perhaps not. But she's one of *them*. They're all the same, aren't they? All full of hate and revenge. All violent and merciless. When has Kyra ever given that impression, though?

'Whatever.'

Kyra grows tired of waiting for any kind of response and pulls her knees up to rest her forehead against them. She almost died earlier, surely she deserves more than spiteful comments and stone cold interactions? It's a dangerous path though, thinking that any of them can be different.

'I'm... sorry.' Kyra looks up at the words, her expression full of the jostling crowd of questions she's likely holding back. 'This is difficult for me. I've been alone for a long time. That's because of your kind. Because of humans. I find it hard to act civil towards you because you're one of them and they took a lot from me. Everything, really.'

Silence rings between them for a collection of seconds. The grinding of the herbs stops. 'One of us made a mistake. A terrible mistake. The humans wouldn't forgive us for it and they came. They came for revenge. They came with violence. When they were done, nothing remained. No one remained. Except me. They took everything from my antlers to my kin. So I took away the bridges.'

And then Kyra screams.

CHAPTER 10

Our Offered Hand

Mistake. Revenge. Violence. Bridges. The words present as a cacophony of tolling bells in Kyra's mind, and she lets out a short scream of surprise as her memories clack back into place all at once and consume her. They rush through the synapses of her brain. Neural water spewing from a broken dam. Racing back to their rightful compartments and coursing through her whole body as they return. She scrambles off the raised platform of the bed and lands on all fours while her mind burns. A forest fire of recollection.

It doesn't last long. Thank goodness for small mercies. Hopefully she never has to feel that again. Panting and sweating she looks to Dennira who half-rises to help her then thinks better of it, apparently. Kyra readies a snipe but all that leaves her mouth is:

'I remember why I'm here.' She tries to straighten up but sways to the side in a tumult of dizziness. Light but weighted at the same time. The clop and scrape of hooves echoes in the cave and a hand catches her shoulder and holds her steady. Dennira can move quickly when she wants to.

'Sit down. It can feel strange when the effects of memoracles wear off.'

Kyra sits against the bed this time, leaning back and waiting for the world to settle and the colours to go back to normal. Dennira backs off and waits patiently. Kyra tries to sort through all the information that's been returned to her. She wades through it, trying to organise it all, and it gradually starts to make sense again. A cold sweat wraps itself around her feverish skin. There's so much. So much she's meant to say. So much riding on her while she's here.

'How long have I been here on the shores?'

'Several hours at least, perhaps nearing half a human's daylight hours.'

'Hmmm. The longest dad's ever made a tether last is just over a full day. I don't have that much time.'

'Your father?'

Kyra takes a deep breath, wanting to be certain she has everything straight in her head first. Having seen Dennira's previous reactions, she can't help but be apprehensive about revealing why she's been sent here. But she has to. It all comes down to her. This might be the only chance they get. She tries to begin, but her mouth turns into the underside of a dirty rug and she coughs. Dennira makes a hand gesture and a glass receptacle appears. She offers it forward, but Kyra hesitates.

'It's just water.' Despite everything, Kyra feels trust and truth in the words of the pathmaster. She's been harsh, but never deceptive. If anything she's been too honest. 'I don't blame you if you don't trust me.'

'Thank you.' The water is crisp and fresh, unlike any water she's tasted in her own world. If crystal turned to liquid it might taste like this. The clarity seems to pass from the taste into Kyra herself, refreshing her and lending her energy. How will she ever explain all of this? She has to try either way.

'I grew up on stories of your kind, you know. My grandmother had a sketchbook and she filled it with drawings. You look a bit different than her sketches, though. In all her drawings there were these grand antlers much bigger than yours, and always covered in beautiful blue flowers and green leaves. Like you were the embodiment of nature or something. She said she once spent several weeks among you, and that you were gentle and wise creatures.'

The memory danced in Kyra's mind and she felt a smile rising. The afternoons spent looking at the sketchbook with her dad are some of her favourites. He would unspool the most wondrous stories about these remarkable creatures. Dennira seems to be listening carefully, her brow creased as she kneels completely still several feet away. It's hard to tell what she's thinking or feeling. Kyra continues, not expecting any kind of response.

'My dad is a magus, same as me, but we aren't like some of the others. I know in the past the other magi worked to create some kind of tether magic to come here. I remember... being told about the war now. But my dad never liked to talk about it in much detail. Never told stories of it. He'd only say it was disgraceful. That the magi had gone too far and that it had cost us all very dearly. Then he'd go right back to telling stories about your kind.

'He's always worked to calm the hatred the magi have towards you and yours. Always tried to talk them round and fight against the stories that they spread. It means we've pretty much lived as outcasts in the magi world. My whole life, and many years before me too.' She couldn't stop herself from talking, it all kept flowing as though rehearsed a thousand times.

'My mother was a magus as well. She worked with my dad to try and fight for your kind. To beat back the campaign of hate that keeps resurfacing. Between them they've helped rid many of their hate, helped them see reason. But she was killed by other magi when I was very young simply for standing up for the pathmasters and trying to advocate for peace.

'She was beautiful. You remind me of her a little actually. But her hair was dark brown and curly, though not as curly as mine. Dad managed to save me and get us out. We've kind of lived in hiding ever since. He's taught me a lot and we've been working on other forms of tether magic that are nothing like those used in the war. I know why I'm here now.' She smiles at Dennira who gives no reaction in return. The pathmaster is totally frozen, rapt with apprehension. Eventually she speaks.

'I'm listening.'

Kyra takes another deep breath, unable to keep her rising hope and excitement off her face. This is what she was sent here to ask. Another minute slips by as she prepares the words.

'I was sent here to try and broker peace between the humans and the pathmasters. Sent to ask if you would consider reopening the bridges once more. Rebuild the broken pathways and allow human souls to pass through your shores again.'

Dennira becomes even more still, if that's possible.

If anything, she bristles. Small and sudden, and almost imperceptible. The blindfold stares back, blank and unrevealing. Kyra realises just how much humans rely on their eyes for expression and understanding.

'What?' It's a short sound that wipes away Kyra's smile just a tad. The pathmaster spoke through her teeth. That's not a good sign. Kyra continues.

'The magi aren't all like the ones that came and brought war with them. Some are different, like me and my dad. We want to rekindle the relationship between the two plains. We're on your side in this and have always fought back against the hateful campaigns of the other magi. I was sent to try and bring back the start of peace between us.

'I know it won't be easy, I know it won't be instant, but the magi of the past made a horrible mistake that we want to correct. Human souls now… because they can't pass on, they hang and linger. They remain anchored before they eventually turn to dust because they can't pass to another world to live again. It's starting to corrupt the planet, blocking the magic pathways. That's not even the main point. The point is that we want to offer an olive branch, to work to gain your trust again and return things to their natural order. We want to move forward. Together. Will you take our offered hand?'

CHAPTER 11

The Ruins of Our Island

All of Kyra's words buzz and flicker around Dennira. Pinching and snapping at her skin with serrated beaks. The girl asks the question in such a simple way. Speaks of the events of the past as though they're small and inconsequential. Does she really think she can just crash-land on the beach and ask for peace? A prickling snakes through her gut. They dare come and ask for the bridges to be remade? They dare come and ask for reconciliation? Sending a young girl to be their mouthpiece, using her as a shield, claiming that things have changed? The prickles turn to sharp needles.

Kyra's smile dulls with every passing second. Concern starts to bubble in her eyes the longer Dennira stays quiet, but how can she possibly respond? This is the last thing she expected to hear from a human, especially in such a casual manner. She can't just wipe away history. Bury it in the sand and open the pathways again because keeping them closed is interfering with their magic. With their souls. What did Dennira stand to gain from this so-called peace? She tries to push out a response, but so many have grouped in her throat that none of them can get out. So she says nothing and turns away, not recalling when she stood up.

How can she trust any of what Kyra said? Even if her tether is a different colour to those used by the humans who came for revenge and violence. Her tether seems stronger, and born of magic with a better intent. Could she be telling the truth? Dennira turns Kyra's words over again and again and catches on certain sentences.

"You look a bit different than her sketches, though. In all her drawings there were these grand antlers much bigger than yours, and always covered in beautiful blue flowers and green leaves. Like you were the embodiment of nature or something. She said she once spent several weeks among you, and that you were gentle and wise creatures."

There's no explanation for how Kyra knows what Dennira's kind are meant to look like. The antlers with the blue flowers is a true detail. Then something tugs at Dennira's memory. A human that spent several weeks among them. A smiling face drifts to the surface of her mind. It's been a long time since she thought about this woman. A stark reminder that humans didn't always stoke feelings of rage in her. She didn't always tar them all with the same brush.

It's in that moment that what Kyra says rings true, and Dennira can't help but smile from under her shock and outrage. This woman was Kyra's grandmother? The resemblance is slight, possibly distorted by the annals of time and fading of memory, but it's not implausible.

The woman in question did spend a few weeks among the pathmasters. Back in the height of co-operation and friendship between humans and the Shores of Separation. Her tether never detached from her body and so her fading never began. A soul can't cross a bridge if there's any connection left to their true body, except in very rare conditions. Her body was in a coma, but her spirit was strong and robust.

She brought light, joy and kindness with her wherever she went. Befriended many of the pathmasters while her soul was stranded here on the shores. Dennira had considered her a respected friend, and often wondered what happened to her after her soul returned to her body. Apparently she spent her life spreading positive and wonderful tales about Dennira's kind. She's grateful for that, but that's not enough to excuse what the other members of her species decided to do.

'Is peace not what you want?' She almost forgot about Kyra, but that is the wrong question to ask, and Dennira finally finds her voice even if she can't look at the girl.

'It's not so simple as what I want. I would have preferred there to be no war between us in the first place.' She tempers her words as the memories flash in gruesome snapshots. Kyra blanches and her face turns pensive. 'What you ask isn't possible. I appreciate that you and your family have always defended us, but it's not enough to wipe away what the rest of your kind did or to mend the rift between our plains.'

'You won't ever consider it?'

Dennira whirls around to face the impetuous teenager in a flare of poorly bridled anger.

'You think I haven't considered it? You think I've never wondered what it would be like to have peace? To open up the shores again and reconnect to the magic that gave me life and purpose? For my existence to mean something again? To see the layered colours and hear the hidden chimes of the universe the way I am supposed to again? I've had more than enough time to consider these things.

'To do as you ask and take your offered branch of peace would be like forgiving the ones who came here with nothing but violence in their hearts and minds. It would be like I was forgetting what they took from me. Who they took. The day I destroyed the bridges I vowed never to open them again. I cut the tether on behalf of my kin to protect them, blinded myself to my own magic, and you ask me to hand-wave the slaughter we faced and set it aside like a stained but empty plate. Satisfied and ready to wash it clean.'

Kyra looks horrified.

'No, of course that's not what we're asking. Forgiving shouldn't require forgetting. That's just dismissal. We simply want to start rebuilding the relationship between the two plains. The two species. To start trying to move on from-'

'From what?' Dennira's brow creases and her face darkens, twisting with bristling rage at every word. 'Move on from the annihilation of my kin? Move on from the humans' inability to listen or forgive? I am the only. One. Left. I watched my herd die. I searched the ruins of our island for those who might have lived, and those who had asked me the kindness of helping them die. I nearly died myself from the energy it took to break my pact. You expect me to move on from this?' She reaches for deeper breaths than she feels she can take. Trying to push the memories down, pack them away, to stop them overrunning her. Spilling out to stain the world red.

'It can end with you, if you're willing to-'

'I have had to end it once before. It shouldn't be my responsibility to do so again.'

'What do you mean?'

Dennira makes a grabbing gesture and her staff flies across the cave into her palm as though dragged by a magnet. Kyra's eyes grow wide. The base of the staff clangs against the stone floor and a cold wind blasts out in all directions.

'Enough. You can't possibly understand it. You clearly only know half the story, and you're not listening. You're not well enough informed to be here asking this of me. Sent by someone who can't even speak of the truth to you. Who has shielded you from it and can't stomach it. You and your kind are here for selfish reasons. To unclog the flow of your dead.

'They should have sent someone else. Someone better versed in the events of the war who wouldn't come here casually asking for decades-old links long broken to be repaired in the simple grasping of a hand. You're not fit for the duty you've been given. You don't know what transpired-'

'Then tell me!' Kyra looks surprised at the power in her own voice and Dennira is cut off. Taken aback by the sharp edges of the words. Kyra stands, facing Dennira head-on. 'Stop talking around it and tell me the story. Tell me your side. Stop spitting hate for a minute and help me understand. I know I'm young, but I'm not stupid. I might not know the full story of the war, but I've felt enough of its effects to be an advocate for ending it.

'You're not the only one who lost people because of it. Plenty of humans were lost, too. No one's ever heard the pathmasters' side of things. If nothing else I could take that back and share it and carry on correcting the misinformation the magi are spreading. I can't do that unless you stop hissing at me and start sharing. If I'm ignorant then inform me. That shouldn't be your job, I know, but I've no other way to learn. Not now. That's our fault. If I still don't understand then I won't ask again.'

If Kyra could see under Dennira's blindfold then she would see her rapidly blinking in disbelief. The girl has strength, that much is certain. Dennira can't find anything to disagree with.

She's never been offered a chance to share her experience. Never been listened to. Always been discredited since the events that sparked the war. Pathmasters were painted as liars and manipulative, power-hungry, incompetent beings. This girl wants to listen, to know the truth only Dennira can tell despite the venom she has spat at Kyra since she arrived. This means Kyra doesn't take her own kin's word as law. As default. That's a first. But is that enough?

'Your kind haven't listened in the past, why is this different? Why would you believe me now when our word has counted for nothing before?' More venom. Dennira can't help it. Permanently defending and distrusting. It's automatic. Her tongue wags at sharp angles of its own accord.

'Because I'm not the same as the others. Nor are we all the same. We're all different. I wasn't part of the war and I don't excuse it. I'm willing to listen. I'm willing to hear your side. If you don't think I understand what I'm asking, then help me. Help to change that.'

For the briefest of seconds Dennira's throat clutches and she pushes down the thickness that springs there like lichen. Her knuckles ache from gripping her staff so hard. What should she do?

CHAPTER 12

The Unmendable Rift

Dennira's gone quiet. Kyra's muscles ache with tension, waiting and ready to flinch should the pathmaster choose to attack or act on her rage. Her heart thumps against the inside of her chest as she waits for any kind of response. Dennira seems to be in deep thought, or shock, or trying to best decide how to dispose of Kyra.

She goes back over everything she said to the pathmaster, how she said it, just in case she's put a foot wrong. She's asked for peace, and she knows it's a big ask, but didn't expecte the anger. Perhaps that's her mistake. As the memories trickle back in a gentle stream it's hard to keep them straight. But with every minute that passes she feels more at ease in one way. All her knowledge of the pathmasters returns, along with her memories of working with her dad to develop the tether magic they're using.

They've been working on the magic since she turned fourteen, or at least that's when she was first really able to help with it. They've never stayed in one place for too long, always on the run from the other magi who chase them. She's never been able to understand why they've been so heavily persecuted just for spreading the truth. A truth the other magi have never wanted.

They've spent the last thirty years doing everything they can to try and drum up support for their cause. It's like they long for another war. They've had some success with recruiting, but what they haven't had success with is creating the correct type of magic to help them travel by tether again.

She only realised in the past year or so that that's probably the reason they're now hunting her dad with a renewed fervour. At first it was just slander, destroying their home no matter where they made it, turning people against them, but now? Now they're changing tack. It was a few years ago that her dad crafted the magic correctly, and they tested and refined it together. They never found out who informed the other magi of their success. They cut everyone out of their lives apart from each other after mum died. They were betrayed by someone they didn't even know. That only made her dad more determined.

Her dad is the best man she knows. His broad smile is infectious, his embrace comforting. She's never been short of encouragement. He's open about nearly everything, including her mother's death, and they speak of her often. Keeping her memory alive between them. Laughing over the good times, crying over the bad. When she was younger he'd sit her on his knee and cuddle her and tell her that she's strong and beautiful, just like her mum. And that she has the best of both of them in her.

She's the perfect melding of their contrasting skin tones, mum's light meeting dad's dark, and she carries the knowledge that she represents them both with pride. Her mother's deep brown eyes, her father's height. Her mother's elegance and her father's strong aptitude for magus skills. He used to joke that they had no idea where her wonderful hair had come from, with its endless volume and tight curls, but then he'd laugh and say it was a gift from her grandmother. And her intelligence and kindness came from them both.

When she thinks about it, it's like he's always trained her to be a peace envoy, and she wouldn't have it any other way. But Dennira is right, if there really is missing information why wouldn't he have shared it?

At first he was hesitant about getting her involved in testing the magic, but he also needed to be confident that he could send and sustain her soul, as well as maintaining the connection while she was away so she didn't drift.

It took many experiments. Took her to many places. Put her in several dangerous situations. She wouldn't change it though. Ever. She wants to help. To reach out to help her dad achieve his goal, because it's become her goal too.

Before she was sent here they'd recapped all the information she'd need to know to get home. Neither of them had expected her to land so close to the sea, there must have been some kind of mix up with the landing spot. Dennira is still silent, absorbed in her own thoughts. Whether good or bad there's only one way to find out.

'I… I remember how to get back now. I have to call up the tether so I can see it and then pull on it a few times, and he'll know to take me back to my body. If I've been here a while already I guess that will have to be soon.'

Dennira lifts her chin just a little, regarding Kyra. If only she could tell what the pathmaster was thinking.

'If you still don't want to consider my offer after you've told me the story I'll go and leave you be.'

No response. A flicker of annoyance buzzes through Kyra but she has to contain it. Getting mad will make matters worse. The situation is delicate enough and Dennira is already perched on a hair trigger when it comes to anything to do with humans or reconciliation, or peace. Or most things, actually.

'I wish you'd answer me somehow, just any kind of indication of what you're thinking. I can't tell in the slightest through that blindfold. Why do you wear it anyway?' Silence. Emptiness. Awkwardness. 'I'm not asking for a definitive decision. How could I? It's a big choice. I'm just asking for a chance. A chance to build trust. For me to come back here again even if only to talk with you. For company. For conversation. So we can start building some kind of link. Some kind of understanding. That would be more than enough, and that's all I'm asking. A step on the road towards peace, not an immediate acceptance of it.'

Dennira moves so suddenly that Kyra gasps. She raises her arms to protect her face, but Dennira walks away. Slowly stepping across the cave. Her staff thunking in between her hoofbeats. Kyra's failed. She came for one thing and she's failed. Dennira is done with her, washing her hands of her. Leaving the olive branch to fall into the chasm. The unmendable rift between their species.

In that moment Kyra is unspeakably angry. Not at Dennira, but at her own kind. Her dad never spoke much about the war, and that's the one thing she needs to know more about if she's being sent to reconcile off of the back of it. Her throat starts to ache and she swallows against the rising sadness. She wants to reach out to Dennira, plead for her to wait, but the pathmaster keeps walking. Her solemn steps echoing.

Then… she stops, and half turns back to Kyra.

'I will tell you my story, but it will be easier if I show you. If you truly want to understand it, you have to experience it yourself. Would you be willing to do that?'

Kyra swallows again against her relief and her new fear, her heart skipping beats as freely as children skipping ropes.

'I… would.'

Dennira motions for her to follow, and Kyra does.

CHAPTER 13

Do Not Fear the Flame

Dennira leads Kyra out of her home and the young girl follows tentatively. She's unsteady on her feet at times, but she's determined, that much is clear. Maybe even a bit stubborn beneath that overly-curious demeanor. Anyone would think she's Annika's long-lost relative, but Dennira can't continue having a soft spot for her because of her similarities. She has to keep protecting her home, and keep her promise to her kin.

No human has ever asked to hear her side of the story. With a rolling, sad lurch it dawns on her that she's never given them the chance. After she severed the connection to the human world, the first human soul that chanced to wash up on her shores in error wasn't even given a second to speak. Sometimes she thinks about it, convincing herself he wasn't scared and that he was there for more violence and accusation. Part of her can't remember which answer is true anymore, she just sees herself snapping his tether. Killing him. In a boiling slew of rage.

So far Kyra is different. She treats Dennira like another person, even before she remembered the history her father told her about. Peace. Is that really the goal? Or is Kyra just here to deceive Dennira into opening the pathways again, rebuilding all the bridges for the humans' own sakes?

Things are different now, there's only her to do the duty of her lineage. If the paths were reopened it would be a tremendous amount of work to lead all the souls on alone. Is she even capable of that? With broken antlers and being so out of practice, she can't honestly be sure. Yet… it would allow her to reconnect with the magic of her ancient duty. Return a part of her that's been missing ever since she blocked it out and renounced it. Leaving nothing but a cold and hollow space deep inside her that longs to have its purpose back.

Who would refuse the chance to become whole again? Now isn't the time for such questions, though. First she has to see if Kyra can handle the truth of things.

They make slow progress on the uneven terrain of the cliff's path, though Kyra manages surprisingly well. She's a buzzing ball of inquiry, but Dennira would rather ask questions of her own than face another battering from Kyra's curiosity. She speaks back over her shoulder, startling Kyra into tripping over a jutting rock, though she keeps her balance.

'You say your father was well-versed in my kind. I know of the magus who started the smear campaign against us. He was the start of it all. Locked in twisted grief. But what did your father teach you of us?'

Kyra's eyes light up with a smile, just for a moment, as she pulls forward her father's lessons.

'I loved his stories of you. It's true that the magus spread a lot of lies. He tried to convince people that you're evil. That you consume souls, trick them into leaving their bodies early. Mutilate them and then return them to their world on purpose to twist their bodies. But dad always said that's all lies.'

Dennira shudders at the stories, seeing clearly how the truth became something else. Something malicious. She shakes away the goosebumps that raise on her skin, and waits for the silver fur on her legs to stop standing up on end. Kyra continues.

'He said you welcome souls to your shores when the bodies they belong to are between the boundaries of life and death, and that pathmasters can open bridges to any world in the universe. He said that every soul's destination is different, each bridge leading to many places. That you work it out by reading the soul's core, only letting them pass over their bridge when it's certain that the tether to their true body has been cut.

'Is what he said true? Do you really guide souls like that? If souls get to relive their lives in other worlds do you ever meet the same one more than once?' This girl is so full of questions that Dennira half expects her to start to deflate with each one she asks, as though they are the source of her life energy and nothing else. She has to stop the stream, and try and keep her attention focused with questions of her own.

'I did. I used to. We used to, but not anymore. Not for a long time. Why did your father not believe the words of the magus?'

'They differed so much from the stories grandma told, and he always said the magus had his reasons. He said something had a hold of him, and was twisting his view of the world. That sometimes things happen to people that makes them unreliable to themselves and, if the circumstances are tragic enough, it changes them forever. He said the magus couldn't let go of what happened to him, so he didn't live in truth anymore.'

The stark image of a young boy burns in Dennira's mind for a fleeting instant, and nausea rocks her. His face is plastered with the creases of fear, his feet glued to the bridge by dread alone. The magus did indeed have his reasons.

'Dad's stories were always more logical, and much kinder. He said they came from grandma's journal that accounted the time she spent here while she was ill. I read her words myself when I was old enough to understand. Whichever pathmasters she met, they sounded elegant and regal, kind and compassionate, and so knowledgeable that she would have happily spent months learning from them.

'Grandma loved to learn, always seeking new knowledge. She was very easily fascinated. Sometimes dad says that she passed down all the questions she never got to ask to me because I ask so many.'

Kyra half rolls her eyes and half laughs at the idea, blushing slightly as she walks.

'The path gets a little narrow from here, but it's short,' Dennira warns.

'It's already a little narrow, how do you walk along it so easily?'

'I've lived here for centuries, and my body is better... adapted.'

'Centuries! Have you really lived that long? Better adapted how? Is your blindfold magic or something?'

Dennira turns quizzically, tilting her head at the teenager and lifting a leg to show her hoof.

'Oh... sorry. I forgot.'

'Don't the antlers give me away? Do humans always project their own anatomy on to others?'

'Sorry, sorry. Oddly enough I was looking at your top half while I was talking to you rather than staring at your legs.'

Something bubbles deep inside Dennira. Something she doesn't recognise at first, and something she doesn't want to rise to the surface. It feels warm and bubbly, and it tries to change the muscles on her face, but she pushes it down.

'You've asked about it so many times now. The blindfold doesn't block my general sight, I can see just fine. It blocks… other layers of things I used to need to see. Things I don't need to see anymore.'

'Woah.' Kyra stares in wonder for so long that Dennira shifts in discomfort.

'Your father is correct about us. Your grandmother must have recorded her experiences here at great length and in great detail.'

'She had a flair for writing, but she was also an artist. The drawings she did were so beautiful I used to stare at them for hours.'

Dennira finds herself wanting to see them for herself, so that she can remember the once-grand splendour of her own kin. Before they were reduced to her and her alone. As a representative of her species sometimes she doesn't feel adequate enough.

'I'm glad there is someone fighting to tell the truth about us. Our duty is millenniums old, and you have the right of it. We met the souls that passed from bodies that were hovering at the border of life and death. When we were sure the link to their old plain was broken we would take them to a bridge. A soul generates its own bridge, its own unique destination, and we just open it when it's ready to let it cross. If we send two souls across the same bridge, they don't end up in the same place.'

'Where do they go?'

'On to other plains to live again, as you said. Each plain has its own system for guiding errant souls, so once they've crossed a bridge they never come back here. No spirit lives on the same plain twice.'

'So you only care for the souls from one plain. Are there many others?'

'Yes. A near endless amount.' Dennira senses another question brewing and quickly cuts across it. 'We're here. This is the Ingress.'

Kyra bites back her question to peer down the curved path.

'I can't see anything.'

'Follow the path down, it's a space inside the cliff, like my home.'

They make the gentle descent and Kyra gasps as they enter the calming space. The only sound is the rhythmic frothing of the waterfall and the lapping of its ripples across the small pool.

'There's grass and flowers in here? How?'

'You should stop thinking of this world in terms of your own.'

'Fair point. It's beautiful here. Like some kind of spa.'

'It's a place for reflection and to be open in and of yourself. No human has ever been here before. Please respect your unique position and take care in how you act here.'

'Thank you for trusting me.'

'It's the only way to show you what you want to see. You may not thank me once we're done. You're certain you wish to proceed?'

Kyra hesitates, perhaps feeling the gravity of what she's asked settle upon her. It's about time.

'Y-yes. I'm sure. Every side of a story deserves to be told. I can't ask for something from you without truly understanding what it means to you first. I know that now.'

Dennira stares at her. She's more mature than she knows already. If Dennira were to remove her blindfold and look at the girl's path, she's sure she'll see an inspiring woman at the end of it. Annika would have liked her.

'Alright. Behind the falling water you'll find the Ingress. It's shaped like a half-moon so it's easy to lie in. Climb into it and calm yourself, and let me know when you're prepared to start the showing.' Kyra does as she's asked, taking small and careful steps behind the curtain of water via a thin path tracing the edge of the pool. 'And Kyra?' Her wide eyes slide around to look at Dennira. 'Do not fear the flame.'

CHAPTER 14

Shoals of Shadows

Don't fear the flame? What does that mean? Kyra's heart clatters about. Dennira stands at the end of the only path out, and a curtain of water blocks Kyra at every other turn. Claustrophobic thoughts press against her as she tries to figure out what's coming.

The pathmaster tilts her head to the side then back and Kyra struggles to hear her words over the rushing water, but she just about makes them out.

'Stop panicking. The flames won't harm you so long as you accept them calmly and are open to the truth. You have my word. Shall we proceed?'

Kyra bites back the compulsion to roll her eyes at her own unfounded panic. She trusts Dennira. Repeatedly reassured herself of that fact. She trusts her. Yes, she's threatened her life, but she's also saved it. Taken her into her home despite her prejudice against Kyra's kind. Sure, she is angry too, but by the sounds of it shc has true cause for that. Kyra is about to find out for herself.

'Yes. I-I'm ready.'

'Lie back and try and focus on accepting the truth.'

Kyra does as she's asked, the smooth stone chilly against her back. She doesn't lie completely flat, but is cradled by the gentle half-moon dip of the Ingress itself.

She can still see Dennira at the end of the path, but as she relaxes into the groove she feels a deep rumbling. A vibration through the rock rippling through her. It's the water. The rhythm of something purely natural, and it's coursing through her, connecting to her. There's something reassuring about it, and her worries melt away with that churning pattern of vibration.

Her mind slows down, all the clamouring questions falling aside as she tunes into that desperately low rumble. There's something special about this place. Maybe even something sacred. Does Dennira believe in gods? She must ask before she goes home.

Dennira nods, perhaps seeing that Kyra has attuned to the space she's lying in, and Kyra nods back. She can trust Dennira. She can. She will.

'This is the easiest way to show you the past. I hope you're prepared, for it won't be easy. I'm passing my memories of the events to you directly. They will become your experiences for a short while. Try not to fight them, I will be watching over you from here.'

Dennira claps the base of her staff against the ground in front of her, and as she takes her hands away it stays standing unassisted. With several fluid gestures that flow in circles around her torso she raises a gentle wind around herself. Both hands rest on her chest, one overlapping the other slightly, and then Dennira slowly begins to pull them away. Something comes with them.

Kyra only sees the light from it at first, a deep blue of midnight like Dennira's robes, but it's flickering. Dancing in a flowing but shy manner. It comes through Dennira's chest at her beckoning and replaces the light blue flame that forever burns on her staff. Kyra is transfixed by it, watching the melding hues of the flame as they twist and play.

The pathmaster raises the staff out of the ground with a tenderness Kyra hasn't yet seen in her. Every movement of her body is soft, and she wills it forward, leaning the silver weapon in Kyra's direction and pushing the flame towards her with her free palm. Kyra has to keep calm, and uses the thrum of the rock to anchor her fear. She asked for this, and she will accept it. The blue orb tracks towards her, bobbing up and down like a languid sprite.

'Raise your palm to it, Kyra.'

She doesn't even take her eyes off the flame as Dennira speaks. She can't. It's too beautiful yet ominous. Her body obeys Dennira's instructions and her arm shakes slightly as the flame draws closer. Inch by inch. She has to accept it. She wants to accept it. She promised she would. She fights back against every instinct her body exerts on her. It screams at her that fire is dangerous and that it's going to burn her and maim her and that she should pull away to protect herself, but she doesn't move. Her trust for Dennira will be proven with this. Her nervous system fires at random, trying to trigger a flinch or a withdrawal and she fights it.

Then the flame touches her hand. It's warm. It has intent. Is it asking for entry? Three times it pushes against her palm. Knock. Knock. Knock. She nods. The temperature gets a little warmer, but doesn't become hot. It glides along the skin of her arm. Her clothes don't singe and her flesh doesn't peel back. It's like bathwater. Pleasant and submerging. Dennira blurs in the distance and Kyra's arm falls back to her side as the flame takes the rest of her body, and drags her mind down into the depths of someone else's past.

Distant voices echo and colours swirl like shoals of shadows. They mould together to form images and pictures and gradually solidify. A timelapse of a painting, becoming more realistic with every brushstroke. Then Kyra is looking through someone's view. It takes her a few moments to realise, or rather remember, that it's Dennira's.

She's on the island. She recognises the lull of the strange sea, but she's much higher up on the cliffs and dangerously close to the edge. She doesn't feel scared, though. This place is home. She knows every divot of its landscape. There's nothing to fear.

These feelings aren't Kyra's. They override her own, and she opens herself to them completely. A catch releases somewhere in her mind and a consciousness mingles with hers, vying for space. If you were to ask her whether she is Kyra or Dennira at this moment, she wouldn't be able to give you a definitive answer.

Then it dawns on her why Dennira wears a blindfold. The world's colour is so bright and rich it's almost blinding. The sky above is laden with golden strings moving through starlit currents. Multicoloured plumes attached to them like celestial balloons. Is this what she sees without the strip of cloth binding her true sight? Kyra catches herself. She is there to learn, not question. And so she watches.

The view turns and another pathmaster comes into the frame. The only other Kyra has seen aside from Dennira and the ones in her grandmother's sketches.

She has her full antlers, the bone-white ivory stark against her black hair which fans out into an afro at the back of a complicated criss-cross of braids that adorn her scalp. Her skin is a complete contrast to the alabaster white of Dennira's. A rich and dark brown that coats her body without a single blemish, and transitions seamlessly into a sleek black fur that covers her deer-like legs under a robe of forest green. Her eyes are the deep colours of the night, but shine with their own starlight.

She's crouching and conversing with a young boy who can't be more than five or six. Her slightly rounded face is animated in conversation with the child, who laughs at something she says. Their rapport could be that of mother and child. Or aunt and nephew. The boy has a glowing aura and a glittering tether that reaches into the ground.

A flood of affection blooms in Kyra as she looks at the other pathmaster and she instantly knows who she is. There's a longing, and beneath that a bond so strong it need never be questioned. It's like nothing she's ever felt. That certainty. That stark truth that this person is hers and will never belong to anyone else. Her view moves towards the pair and a playful spark zips through her. The young soul dashes off to chase a fluttering moth.

'You're a natural with him.' Kyra feels Dennira speak through her.

'I'm definitely better with the younger ones than you, that's for sure.'

'I'll have you know I'm very maternal when I want to be.'

'That'll be the day.'

They chuckle at each other and the other pathmaster

briefly puts a hand to Dennira's cheek. Her skin sparks under her touch and Kyra rides a wave of happiness.

'Is he going to be crossing?' Dennira asks.

'I think so. His core had a tentative link for a while but I'm fairly certain the connection is fading. I'll summon his bridge soon. I hate when they come here so young.'

'Me too. It feels like he's barely had chance to live.' Dennira's fingers interlace with those of the other pathmaster. As they watch him, the tether running into the ground flickers, and with a quiet spark it vanishes. They wait, conversing and playing with the child for while after the tether disappears. Finally Annika stands straight and nods. It is time.

'Hopefully his next life will be longer. Joel? Come on, honey, let's summon your bridge.' The young boy returns to her without hesitation, his face alight with joy and trust. The three of them make their way to two stone pillars with intricate carvings. They're dangerously close to the edge of the cliff. A gate out into the nothing above the sea. 'Alright now, you stand here in the middle and we'll light the torches.' With her own staff, silver like Dennira's but with a differently shaped crook and carvings, she conjures a blue flame and kneels to hold it in front of the boy. There isn't a trace of fear in him. You'd think he'd been here many times before.

'Why do you have flowers on your head?' He asks as she offers the flame to him.

'For the same reason you have two arms and two legs. It's just how I'm made.'

'Can I have flowers on my head too?'

'Well, I'm not sure. Maybe if you look after yourself

properly you'll be able to bloom one day.'

'Really?'

'Really. Here, you can take one of mine.' The pathmaster reaches up to pluck a blue flower from between the foliage on her antlers and places it gently in the boy's eager palm. 'Be careful with it though, they're fragile.'

'Thank you, Anniki.'

'It's Annika. An-nik-a. But well done for using your manners.'

'Annika.'

'That's right! OK, are you ready?' Joel nods, beaming down at the flower in his hand. Annika holds the flame close to his chest and extracts a much smaller one to join it. Then splits the orb in two with a graceful gesture and sends the flames to light the podiums either side of the young soul. A blue flash races across his eyes and he turns to stand on the edge of the cliff as though it's the most natural thing in the world. A pang of sadness sours inside Dennira. He's too young, he's too young, is all Kyra can hear.

After a few moments the pillars begin to glow from top to bottom, and a fine dust gathers in the air. Sheets of carved, transparent rectangles roll out before the boy. Gleaming ropes lacing themselves together to hang them in the air. And it rolls, and rolls out like the endless tongue of a strange beast. The air thickens with the magic and Joel turns, still beaming and cradling the flower, and sets off across the bridge as though he's being called home to his favourite place in the world.

'You were so good with him.' Dennira says again without thinking.

'You've said that once, are you so surprised?' Annika's eyes are bright with amusement.

'No, not at all, I'm just paying you a compliment.'

'Well in that case, thank you. I'll have to try and think of one to give to you in return, but it might take a while.'

'Hey!' Dennira elbows Annika playfully and they turn to watch Joel make the rest of his journey.

There's a flicker. So slight Kyra wouldn't have seen it if Dennira hadn't focused on it so intently that it almost knocks her sick. She stares now, straining her eyes, examining every inch of the boy and waiting. Annika must have felt her bristle.

'What is it?'

Dennira doesn't answer. She's waiting. Hoping. She's wrong, she has to be. But it happens again and this time Annika sees it too. His tether flashes back into view. Swaying like a taper of lost ribbon. It has nowhere to anchor.

'No. No I was so sure. The ties were cut. We waited more than long enough.' Annika's hand covers her own mouth and she shakes her head.

'Joel! Joel, come back.'

'Please sweetie come back off the bridge, now!'

Joel turns, but his smile is gone. Now his eyes are wide. Impossibly wide. The whites big and round, drowning his pupils. The flower is crushed in his fist. Annika makes to step forward but Dennira grabs her arm.

'No, don't. It's too dangerous. It's not your bridge.'

'I know that but we have to get him off there now. I was so sure his connection was gone. I saw it disappear!'

'Joel, come back. Come back!' Kyra shudders at the

desperation in Dennira's voice. The raw pleading. The boy isn't moving. Just staring that horrible, terrified stare. The pillars flare and two orbs shoot towards the boy. They engulf him, and he screams. These flames are not friendly like the ones that swallowed Kyra.

The agony in the young boy's cries is tragic and Kyra feels Dennira's lungs twist and flip in her ribcage. Annika can only gasp and choke back a sob so full of regret that it chimes in Kyra as a deep and hollow bell. None of them can look away. The boy's body jerks and tangles, flickers and flashes, and then the bridge collapses around him and his tether whips upwards, pulling him skyward like a cruelly hooked sea creature. Then he's gone.

The bridge dissipates and silence unfolds between them. Neither seem to be breathing. The seconds slip by and eventually Annika lets out a pained whisper.

'I was so sure. There was no tether. It was gone. He was ready to cross. I was so sure.'

'Annika…'

'I was so sure!' She screams it this time, falling into a crouch with her hands over her face. Her staff clangs against the rocks as concerned shouts echo behind them. Dennira holds Annika tight and rocks her as she cries.

I didn't sense it either. The tether wasn't there, it was gone. It's happened before. We've all struggled to read souls before. It will be OK. It will be OK. He was so young, though. So young. Too young for that. His body in the human world won't…

Then Dennira breaks down too, replaying it in her mind. Kyra experiences every wrenching cry from the two women and the scene fades to black once more.

CHAPTER 15

Monsters Like You

The scene changes and Kyra has to catch her breath, even though she's not in her own body. There's no let up between the visions as another melds into view. They're in one of the settlements before they were destroyed. She can barely believe it's the same one she was trapped in and saved from earlier that day. The homes are functional, small hut-type constructions, and it strikes Kyra how happy the pathmasters are with so little. There's no technology here, no sprawling two-storey homes, hardly any of the commodities of the human world. Yet they're all perfectly content.

The bond of community is so strong that Kyra wishes to hold on to that feeling. They're in the main square of the little village and it's full of life, and full of pathmasters of all shapes and sizes. They're just as diverse as humans, even in this small community. Dennira sits near the fountain, which is working, with Annika and a few others and they discuss the events of what now appears to be a day or so ago. Annika still seems reluctant to smile, her dark eyes haunted by her mistake.

Dennira is about to speak when a disturbance outside the settlement pricks everyone's ears. A feeling of dread blooms in Kyra's chest and Dennira's heart starts to race. She hoped everything would be OK, that there would be no consequence. Immediately the need to protect Annika fills her from top to bottom and shines like a beacon. The dread darkens as a spectre staggers into the settlement. A human spectre. Thoughts batter Kyra's consciousness.

He shouldn't be here. How is he able to come here in that form? Is that a tether? No, it's not a true one, not a natural one. This shouldn't be possible, who is he?

The man looks haggard, ruined and broken. A red light blurs around him and he's clutching his chest desperately. Behind him a fraying tether flickers and flashes in and out of existence. It's spikey and unrefined. Unstable. He's tall, robed in magi attire, and his unfriendly face is tight with discomfort and something darker. Something Kyra can't place. When he speaks, his voice is distorted but clear enough to understand.

'Where is the one who destroyed my son?'

Silence ripples through the pathmasters. Annika stiffens. Dennira grabs her hand and holds it tight. 'Where is the one who made him suffer?' Annika shakes off Dennira's hand and turns to look at her. The things their locked gaze communicates are far beyond Kyra's own understanding, but Dennira's chest goes tight and she stays ready to protect the one she loves. Annika steps forward toward the flickering human, standing tall but cowed by her error.

'Your son was Joel?'

The man snarls, eyes zoning in on Annika. 'It was you?'

'What happened was a deeply regrettable mistake,

and I'm so sorry for it. I was certain his tether to your plain had expired. We waited-'

'I didn't come here for your excuses. Do you have any idea what your mistake did to him? What it did to his body?' His raw tones echoed around the settlement.

No one had an answer. 'His body is twisted beyond repair. His mind is broken. You mutilated him!'

Annika flinches and Dennira longs to go and stand with her, but stays where she is, trusting in the strength of her partner. Still she ponders how this man is actively able to be in both plains at once. The magic he's using has a foul stench and aura. It's like he sent his soul here on purpose while his body remains healthy and living. His soul isn't at the boundary between life and death. It has an unnatural duplicity.

Is that why it's causing him so much pain to be here? Why his tether is so crude and fragile? If he keeps it up he will harm his soul and his body by extension. The look in his eyes tells her that he already knows this, though. That he did it anyway. That it's worth the risk.

'I didn't mean to harm your son. Joel was a good soul, a wonderful child-'

'Don't you dare utter his name to me again. Things like that don't happen by accident. That kind of destruction is never and accident, it's cruel and purposeful. Is that the game you all play here? Use your power to torture the occasional soul for your own amusement and twisted ends?'

Annika's rage can be felt even from a distance. 'I would never assign anyone to the same fate as your son. We tried to call him back from the bridge but he was too scared to move-'

'My son was brave. He had more courage than all of you! He fought his illness for months, and his soul came to you for help and you desecrated it.' The magus spat towards Annika and fell into a fit of violent coughing, clutching his chest tighter. 'You heed my words, all of you. When we have perfected this magic we will return. We will return to make sure that monsters like you never have the chance to twist the souls of humans again. Never have the chance to take the life of someone who could have lived.'

A darkness drips from every word, and not a single pathmaster present doubts his promise. With a cry of pain he crumbles out of existence, returning to his own plain.

Annika folds at the middle, hands covering her eyes, and Dennira runs to her along with several others. Then Kyra feels the familiar pull of the darkness and the scene starts to change again.

Dennira is in the most beautiful cave Kyra has ever seen. Crystals light the place like lamps and Dennira stands in front of a huge shard of clear, glass-like rock that sits at the centre of a rippling pool. Shoals of threads swim languidly around in the air and the pathmaster reaches up to pluck one with nimble fingers.

The large crystal shard comes to life with images and it shows a man kneeling at the bed of a sheet-covered mass, body lurching with sobs violent enough to sound like retches. Kyra is grateful she can't see what or who is under those sheets, and thanks whatever gods might be listening when the pictures shift.

It's the magus that came to the island. Now he addresses a room with passionate and angry fervour.

Something flutters in the back of Kyra's mind, but she struggles to catch it as it's lost among the clamouring worries that swarm in Dennira.

This is the man that threatened Annika. The one who threatened to come back. That awful magic he made, he's sharing it, developing it. Raising an army? That many can't possibly cross over, not before they're treading the boundary of death.

It isn't right. It isn't fair. It was an easy mistake, an accident. Nothing more. Annika doesn't deserve to be scared and guilty and ashamed for one mistake she can't fix. Humans know nothing of our work, of its complexities. I'll protect her. I will. Forever entwined. Forever bonded.

The more Kyra watches the man through Dennira's eyes, the more and more something tugs on her. Yanking with a desperation but also with denial. A realisation swims beneath the surface but she can't yet piece it together. It evades Kyra's grasp constantly, but there's not much time to ponder it as her view lurches yet again.

Dennira comes across the prone body of one of her kin and there's no explanation for their death. In quick flashes Kyra sees the discovery of more and more bodies over time, and then the magus is there again. His tether stronger, and his pain less intense. He carries a weapon with him, and uses it to channel the power of his soul toward another pathmaster.

He flashes up in scene after scene. Eventually more and more unfamiliar figures appear, all wearing the black robes of the original magus. They all glare at the pathmasters with hatred and attack them willingly and on sight. Justice writ plain on all their faces.

Snippets of panicked thoughts nip at Kyra as she watches. They're getting stronger. They've figured out how to bring weapons. They've learned how to extend their stay on another plain. We're under attack.

Then Kyra is shown normal souls. Ones that come to the shores because it's their time to cross. The hatred is in their eyes too. Sometimes fear. Every time Dennira tries to approach a soul to help it they scream and try and flee, or plead for her not to consume her soul or set it alight. They scramble away, refusing to co-operate or listen. The souls aren't passing to their next lives. Some stagger towards the sea in a desperate effort to escape and dark shapes claim them as food.

The magus must be spreading rumours and lies about them in the human world, upsetting the order of things. Costing people's souls the chance to live again elsewhere. His hypocrisy disgusts Dennira, and the flame of anger is stoked and blazes more within her with each and every vision that Kyra has to witness.

An endless number of these images flicker and overlay to paint the grim picture of more than five years of the pathmasters being under near-constant attack by those loyal to Joel's father. So many pathmasters are lost, the settlements dwindle year after year.

Kyra is struck by a wild dizziness as she tries to comprehend all of Dennira's thoughts. They've been well organised and explained, but it's too much for her to take in. The loss, the fear, the anger. The despair at seeing so many of her kin taken, the determination not to lose any more. The nights spent comforting an increasingly distraught Annika, who blames herself for everything that's come to pass.

No comfort is enough to reassure her that her mistake was one that could be understood by all of her kin. She pushes people away over time and Dennira laments, feeling her drifting away on a raft of guilt and a sea of tangled bodies. She can't bring Annika back, but she'd give anything to take away her pain.

Yet as Kyra witnesses all of this she knows it's not the end. With her entire being she hopes that she doesn't have to see any more of it, but also remembers her promise. She has to see what happened, she has to face what her kind did to Dennira, as strong as the denial that's building inside her is.

As strong as the pain of seeing that happen to Joel. This is the truth, and she can't look away from it.

CHAPTER 16

Sever the Ties that Bind

A new vision of the settlement curls into Kyra's mind like smoke. The atmosphere couldn't be more different. Solemn and half-empty, some homes already without occupants. Everyone is weary, and it saddens Kyra just how small a group 'everyone' now means. She doesn't know how much time has passed since the last vision, but doesn't have time to wonder as shouts start to echo in the distance. They come from the direction of the beach where she herself landed on the island, coupled with a foul wind. Dennira and Annika are the first to rise, tempers flaring, and hurry to meet what they can only assume is yet another attack. Their hands interlace as though they'll never let each other go.

I won't lose anyone else, we've lost enough, Dennira thinks. And Kyra feels just how determined she is to make sure that promise rings true. Dennira is strong, Kyra has seen her fight now, and Annika too. They'll protect the others, although every single one of the pathmasters can hold their own. For a moment Kyra is certain that they'll win, but then she remembers why she's here viewing these things in the first place and her stomach tingles and swoops. She can't warn them, she can't help them, because this is all in the past.

The pathmasters pool out onto the grassland that meets the beach and are stunned into silence. Every few seconds another human soul flickers into existence. Their tethers are strong, their bodies solid, almost as though they've physically crossed to this plain. Dancing, dark-red embers seethe in their eyes. They look like blood-lit demons. Some carry weapons, others just carry hate, and Kyra is quickly losing count of the numbers. It's gone past being equal.

The frontman steps forward, his face twisted with malice. Joel's father. Every time she sees him, that familiar feeling darts around and clangs in warning inside Kyra, but he's always too far away or his face too gnarled with disgust and righteousness to pinpoint why.

It could even be one of Dennira's feelings. She can barely differentiate.

'I keep my promises, pathmasters. Our magic is perfected, and we come for vengeance. For my son, and for all those you might have harmed in the past, or intend to in the future.'

His sneer makes Kyra shiver. It doesn't seem human. He turns to his fellow magi. 'Go for their horns! They use them to harm others. You all heard about the remains of the flower that Joel had in his hand when he returned. He brought it back to warn us, to show us how to defeat the ones who wronged him. These monsters must be stopped!'

A cheer erupts from the crowd and Dennira's mind races. None of what he's said makes any sense, he's drawn wild conclusions that have been pulled out of shape and maimed by his grief. There are too many of them. They continue to appear. A sea of robed magi,

102

each and every one convinced that the pathmasters are vicious monsters.

Something shifts in Dennira then, it switches with a heavy metallic clunk. Humans are so ungrateful. All these endless centuries her kind have guided them across their bridges, cared for their souls, been their shepherd. There have been other mistakes, and there will always be more. And for this one single mistake, and the insatiable disdain of one man, all that has been forgotten. Trodden underfoot like so many grains of insignificant sand. They come in force with nothing but violence. They lost one of theirs and so take from others to appease their sadness. These kinds of delusions can only come with a human's imagination and lack of emotional control. She won't allow it. She'll fight. She'll protect as many as she can.

'Into the forests, we have the upper hand here. This is our home and it will stay ours. Protect yourselves, send them back where they came from!' They follow the order without question, it comes from the mouth of a male pathmaster and Dennira's respect for him buzzes through Kyra as they rally on his command. At the same time, the magus shouts his own call to action.

'End their monstrous reign!'

And the battle begins.

The images make little sense but have so much impact. The fierce clanging of weapons meeting, the blasting of magics colliding. The haggard breath of those who run and the shouts of those who don't run fast enough. It's a siege. The pathmasters are outnumbered from the start.

Annika is missing, lost in the fray. They all spread out

to use the terrain of their home to their advantage. Dennira is exhausted as she stumbles across another body. Antlers snapped off, silver blood dripping from them. The worst kind of desecration. Needless. But it isn't Annika. At least it isn't Annika. It's a selfish thought but Dennira doesn't care. Pathmasters bond for life, and bond fiercely. They become completely entwined with their bonded. Something humans will never understand.

A chill sweeps through her. Maybe they do understand. Maybe they understand too well. The magus' bond with his son did this to him. Could Dennira account for her own actions if Annika was... no. Don't think of it. Not now. Nothing could make her an agent of such destruction. Could it?

Searching for their link deep inside her core she panics. Annika is in trouble. The bond flutters like a distressed bird. She has to find her. She springs through the forests, legs burning with the effort of taking endless leaps one after the other. In the peripheries of her vision she catches snatches of fights. The screams of pathmasters and humans mingling and impossible to tell apart.

'Annika?' Shouting is a bad idea but she doesn't care. She calls and calls, waiting for a response or a spark from her bond to tell her Annika is close by. A twinge yanks on her core and she takes a sharp left, heading for the jagged base of the cliffs where they meet the forest. The acrid smell of smoke tinges the air. How have they managed to start fires? They have far too much power for projections of souls. There's no time to ask questions as she skids to a stop in the treeline. All thought stops and Kyra is hit by the silence as though slapped.

Annika is being held on her knees by two magi, and Joel's father circles her in slow, stalking steps. Dennira hasn't been seen… yet. She has the advantage, she can take them by surprise.

'Wait.' The word, gentle as a feather, plants itself in Dennira's mind effortlessly and she stops in her tracks. Annika isn't looking at her, she's looking at the magus. They can talk through their bond as well?

'Why should I wait, I can free you, I can't stand to see them hold you like that I-'

'Just wait, Den. Please. Maybe they can still be reasoned with. Maybe if I just apologise again-'

'That hasn't worked so far.'

'Please. Just wait. Let's just see.'

The link falls silent and with great restraint that boils in all of Dennira's muscles she stays hidden in the treeline as the magus speaks.

'You're the one. The one who mutilated my boy. The one who made him suffer. The one who's torn my family apart. None of them will help me. None of them will help Joel. My wife refuses to blame your kind. My only remaining son too traumatised by the loss of his brother. The honour of being here at my side should be his.' Kyra's breath is knocked from her as the magus speaks. The details. They're too familiar. Too similar. It can't be. It can't be him.

'I can do nothing other than apologise-'

He strikes Annika across the face so hard that Dennira almost darts forward then and there, but she has to wait. She was asked to wait.

It makes sense now. Why her dad never spoke of him. Or anything to do with it. A turbulent nausea crashes against the sides of her stomach over and over. The magus. Kyra knows him now. Knows him without ever having met him.

'Still pretending that it was all a mistake? How pitiful. You refuse to be held accountable. But accountability can be dispensed. You see and hear that? The smoke, the screams? It's all your fault because you won't admit your wrongdoing.'

The magus…

'Stop this, my kin are not to blame for my mistake and I have admitted fault already. I've done nothing other than that ever since it happened.'

…is Kyra's…

'At least you admit your own inadequacy.'

…grandfather.

'I have never had anything but regret in my heart for what happened to Joel.'

It happens so fast that Dennira thinks it's imaginary. At the mention of his son's name, the magus pulls a knife from the belt of his robes and plunges it into Annika's chest. Her eyes wander to meet Dennira's.

'Den… I was wrong again. I'm so sorry. Forever entwined. Forever bon-'

Silence.

Dennira can't stop the word from pouring out of her, nor the rage from rising. Kyra shouts along with her at the zenith of her sickening realisation.

'No!' But then Dennira's face is crashing against the floor, the smell and taste of earth and blood ripe in her nostrils and mouth. Ambushed. She strains to look up, gasping against the crackling dissolution of her bond. 'Annika!'

Kyra is frozen. Horrified. Swirling in a mire of disbelief and borrowed grief. How can this be the truth?

'Take her horns. They hold her power.' Dennira's stomach lurches as human hands seize her antlers. Rough and without care. This is wrong. This is all wrong. Magic flares from the palms of the gripping, mauling hands. The pressure in Dennira's head grows and screeches like nails on porcelain plates and she screams. A primal and raw sound. Sparks dance across her eyes with the snap of every nerve in her body. Crack. Crack. One after the other.

Silver droplets spatter the grass either side of her. The world swims as her antlers are tossed away in front of her. Part of her removed and discarded. They should be attached to her. They're hers. They belong to her. The blue flowers wilt instantly, the foliage curling like burning paper and dissolving. The sides of her face are slick and warm, but her body shivers with cold. She can look at nothing but Annika's lifeless body. Her vitality gone, her strength drained. The light of her beautiful soul that passes to everyone she speaks to muted and betrayed by the emptiness around her. She can't be gone.

The magus smiles. He has the temerity to smile. Dennira's vision sharpens, something dangerous rising from a depth she's never had to explore. One that everyone has but can only hope they never need. It slinks past Kyra on all sides. A nest of dark eels swarming up and out. They whisper of death and destruction. They melt with her own inky tendrils of guilt and regret. Her family did this to the pathmasters. Her own family.

If Kyra could run from Dennira then she would. The thick cloud of emotions rising in the pathmaster broils in a storm and Kyra would rather be anywhere else. The magi can feel it too. Their leader isn't smiling anymore.

Dennira bucks and struggles, emitting grunts and shouts of pure livid hate. When she's free enough she manages to raise the back end of her staff and pushes it straight through the astral flesh of one of her captors, shattering their core and snapping their tether. The other one doesn't last long, either, and the leader begins to back away. Unsure of himself for the first time.

'It's too late to consider your mistakes.' Dennira snarls at him as his back meets the black stone of the cliffs. She slams her staff into the ground and a shining blue circle appears beneath her, adorning itself with carvings and lost tongues of languages that humans will never know. Reaching for something ancient. Something only called for in dire need. Something each pathmaster only gets to invoke once, and once alone. Linked to the magic as old as her pact as a pathmaster.

She struggles to contain her screams as ivory tendrils snake out through the flesh of her back, and knit themselves together. Great wings form, as though made from the antlers she lost, and lift her from the ground an inch or so. She never stops glaring at the magus, who watches in loose disbelief and sizzling terror.

Plucking her staff from the ground she kicks off, shooting skyward, shedding flecks of blood and tears into the sky around her. From up above the island she sees the devastation in its full force. Bodies strewn and turned into crumpled rags, fire eating through her home. Stains mixing like inks and the vacant echo of mindless agony.

This is what they wanted. This is what they'll get.

Through the falling tears that she can't stem she draws symbols in the air around her, her wings unfolding to their full width and pulling at the muscles in her back. The physical toll doesn't matter. She'll pay it tenfold if she has to.

With a shaky voice she speaks as clearly as she can, holding back the riptide of emotion. Her voice booms, covering the island, spreading out into the sky of the whole world.

'The trust between our species has been broken. The connection between our plains must be severed. I renounce the duty of the pathmasters and with it our tolerance of human kind. I hereby sever the ties that bind us!'

She plunges toward the ground, staff raised, face encased in sadness. A great bell tolls as the staff rips into the earth, sending a web of cracks out in a circle around her.

The tethers of every human snap in the same second, and they choke on their surprise as they die. Disconnected from their physical bodies in a split second. Their forms flickering out of existence as easily as they appeared. Annika's killer is no exception.

She looks up to see a colossal bridge fade into view in the sky, and it lights the beacons for every other bridge around the island. A network of pathways so great and uncountable that for a moment Dennira is still in the blue light of their volume. A rumbling shakes the island's core and magic pours from the sky like debris. A single sob escapes her as the bridges begin to crumble, to fall away. The link between this world and the human world retreats into nothing. The gates of all the others sealing themselves behind the barrier of her renounced vow. A lifetime of duty scattered to the winds of hate.

There's no going back now. Even as her vision starts to blur and her wings crack and crumble, she makes peace with her choice. Shaking and full of so many irreconcilable things she crawls towards Annika's body. With a grief-stricken howl Kyra's view fades for the last time.

CHAPTER 17

Loss and Delusion and Denial

Dennira watches over Kyra the entire time she's experiencing the memories. She doesn't need to see them too, she's seen them quite enough, yet she all but relives the progression of events from the reactions in the girl's body. She tried to knit the memories together for Kyra in a way that wasn't too disturbing, playing down much of the damage done to her kin and not showing her unnecessary violence and death. It is still the whole truth, though, and Kyra isn't reacting well. Her whole body goes through phases of twitching and jerking, and she breaks into a sweat about halfway through and shivers intermittently. Her eyes flicker and roll under her closed lids, but soon she'll wake and Dennira is ready and waiting to help her recover.

It's a lot to take on. She didn't think Kyra would actually be willing to learn the truth of the actions of her kind. None have been willing in the past, though in fairness they weren't given that chance. Don't soften towards her too much though, Dennira thinks, whether she's similar to Annika or not. She could still have another agenda or be leading her into a trap or ambush. Perhaps this is over-cautious, but a lack of caution was the problem in the beginning.

She'd been so sure that there would be no consequence for Annika's mistake. So confident because it happened before with other pathmasters and the event would pass unmarked. Souls are tricky things, and even the most experienced elder among the pathmasters could make a mistake if the conditions are right for it. They can only use their best judgement at the time, and the state of the tether of that particular soul in the moment of the reading.

It wasn't worth getting tangled up in it all again. Whether she could have done more to check Joel's tether, read it with more focus and depth, but there was no reason not to trust Annika's skills. Dennira takes a deep breath and focuses on Kyra, who shows signs of waking.

The girl's body moves before her mind has completely returned from the visions of the flame and she scrambles from the half-moon rock. Limbs flail and hoarse yells pour out of her. She sways dangerously with a wild look in her eyes, and silver-tinted tears stain her flushed cheeks. Dennira approaches her calmly and kneels, putting a hand to Kyra's shoulder to steady and still her. Her eyes are empty of everything but the silver glow of the tether, but gradually she comes back to her own mind and her breathing can't seem to choose a rhythm.

Her face fills with the weight of what she's witnessed and dark circles mark the skin under her eyes. Dennira helps her stand, and can feel her shivering as she tries to walk.

'Come with me, Kyra. Let's go to the spring. The water will help you.'

'We… what he did… why. Why would they… there

was no reason to. Why did it have to be him. Why us. Our… my family took yours. My family took yours. My grandfather. Annika didn't mean to. It pained her so much. They took it all.' She trips over her words, each sentence mingling with another and binding together. Dennira bristles, wondering if she misheard the word grandfather. Wondering, but doubting it.

'It's alright, you need to recover before we speak. You've been through a lot.'

'It's you who's been through too much, and my family were responsible.' There it is again. My family. Yet the words bloom a sadness inside Dennira instead of anger. Even if Kyra has a closer link than she realised. Even if it's true. There's one thing that overshadows that fact in that moment.

No other living thing has ever acknowledged Dennira's pain. Her loss. Now, here, a teenage girl is the first. It isn't what she says, but how she says it. Solemn, choked with sympathy and truth. It makes it all weigh even heavier. So long as no one else has ever known it, it hasn't quite been real.

Now it's acknowledged, Dennira realises how she's longed for someone else to validate her anger. Her sadness. To try and have even the slightest understanding of her experience even if they could never truly know. The bitter crystals encasing her heart start to crack and crumble, just a little, but now is the time to focus on Kyra.

She leans heavily on Dennira's arm, unsure of her footing and even less sure of her feelings. Her uncertainty writ plain on her face. The heat of her palms burns through the sleeves of Dennira's robe, and her dark green sweatshirt blooms with damp patches under her arms. They travel slowly down the short path and out from behind the waterfall, around the pool to its edge. Kyra half falls to her knees and slides sideways to sit with her legs bent to one side. For a moment she just breathes, perhaps trying to steady the world. Seeing through soulflames can be quite taxing on non-magic folk, but with Kyra being a magus-in-training she seems to have handled it better than others might.

With a wave of her staff Dennira summons an upturned shell and allows it to fill with a little water from the spring. Kyra pulls at her sweater before managing to remove it, and it lies discarded on the grass.

'Here, sip this slowly. It will help counteract the effects of the flame.'

Kyra does as she's asked. Her eyes now full of not only her presence and the shining glimmer of the tether, but a deep void that can only be achieved with truth. Unwanted, incomprehensible truth. Yet she isn't fighting it. She's not once tried to deny it. For long moments they sit in silence. Kyra sips from the shell every few seconds and stares into a distance that Dennira knows far too well.

It's small, but a pang shoots through Dennira's gut. Did she have to share this burden with someone so young? Should she have refrained? Learning things can change a person in irrevocable ways, and Dennira doesn't want to be responsible for passing too much trauma to a teenager, no matter how grown up her words might sound. Still, what's done is done.

'Are you feeling more grounded?'

'A little. In one way at least. In others... I don't know.'

Kyra's voice is strained, thin and fragile. 'Thank you for the water.'

'Come. We'll get some air. When you're ready, we can talk about what you saw.' The girl nods and pulls her sweatshirt towards her but doesn't put it on. She needs less support than before, but Dennira stays close to hand just in case.

When they make it to the top of the cliffs, Kyra spreads her arms and drinks in the crisp air as it wraps around her. She doesn't smile, that action seems beyond her and rightfully so, but her relief is palpable. Dennira takes her to sit next to Annika's lantern. The lone sentinel at the summit of the island. If anyone can help comfort this girl it's Annika.

'The lanterns are beautiful.' Kyra looks at it reverently as she speaks. 'Why do you light them?' A question. That's a good sign at least.

'They hold the essence of the souls of my kin so long as I keep them alight. It's not much. A mere impression of who they were, but they can communicate in their own way. I keep them alive in a sense this way. I've become their caretaker.'

'And this one is…' she doesn't need to say the name.

Dennira nods and confirms the unfinished statement. 'Yes, this is Annika's lantern.'

A crease forms in Kyra's brow and she studies the object again with her new knowledge.

'She won't mind if I sit with her?'

'Not at all.'

They each take up a space either side of the lantern and Dennira revitalises the flame. Kyra shouldn't be able to hear Annika's words, but she turns her head towards the lantern as though listening. The saddest of smiles paints the girl's lips for all of a second. Even in this situation Annika is trying to comfort her. She's far too kind and gentle to have deserved her fate.

'What happened… after?' Kyra doesn't look at Dennira as she asks, and Dennira doesn't need to ask what she means. She stares out over the island as she responds, trying not to replay the images conjured by the words.

'When I awoke from breaking the bridges and the tethers I searched for my kin. Progress was slow, my whole body felt aflame from using so much power. I'd hoped to find some survivors. I scoured the whole island, but all I found were bodies. One after another. I did find two who were still living. Our apothecary and one of our elders but… it was kinder to help them pass, given their injuries. To try and let them live would have been cruel.'

Dennira gazes up at the belt of souls as they plod along the sky like a swarm of jellyfish. Undulating and pulsing as they travel onward. 'The violence was unspeakable. Some of my kin had been skewered with their own detached antlers. Killed brutally and maimed. It was all so needless and unforgiving.

'Grief can be a dangerous thing. It can make people cruel. Turn them into something else. A creature brought into twisted existence through loss and delusion and denial. It all stirs inside some people like a great cauldron of hate and festers. They have no way to vent it, or don't know how. The root of all this was one man's grief and his inability to cope with it.'

Kyra can't respond, and only stares at the ground in solemn agreement. Dennira looks up at Annika's lantern and feels a warm, reassuring light in her core.

'Annika was a good pathmaster. Very skilled and empathetic. But everyone can make mistakes. She'd never hurt anyone on purpose. It wasn't in her to do such a thing. She regretted what happened with Joel beyond anything else in her life. She was broken by it and I tried to help hold the pieces together. I'm not sure how well I did with that. It was hard to see her so torn up by it, so forlorn.

'The magus wouldn't even listen. He wouldn't hear her apology, or her explanation as to why it might have happened. He didn't care. All he knew was that his son was gone and that Annika, and therefore all her kind, were to blame. He wouldn't stop until he'd acted out the revenge his grief told him would bring him peace. Everything else could be reasoned away.

'That's why I washed my hands of your kind. The ignorance of any truth but the one they believe to be theirs. You have this unending need to spread these truths and make others accept them. That's how he pulled in so many others to his cause. His truth was so strong for him that he made it real for others, and they rallied to it. People sometimes trust the experience of others over their own, before they've had the chance to experience things themselves. I wanted no further part of a duty that would lend our power to such a species. So I broke the bridges and used my energies elsewhere. I became the warden of my kin instead. I created the lanterns and I will keep them burning no matter what.

'I moved up here after I'd taken care of all my kin. The settlement was in too much disrepair for one person to fix and I didn't want to live there alone. The caves are safer shelter. So now you know. You know what this place once was and what it's now become and why. How I came to be left with nothing but the shades of my kin's souls. The keeper for the lanterns of the lost. Now you know exactly what you ask when you ask me for peace.'

CHAPTER 18

Responsibility

Kyra has no idea what to say. All her words are coiled up in the horror of what the flame showed her, and in Dennira's account of what happened after. Any combination of words she tries to link together is feeble and inappropriate. Fragile in the face of all that Dennira's been through. They sit no more than two feet apart, looking out over the island. The desolate place overlaid with echoes of Dennira's memories. A lost vitality fading like colours bleached by the sun.

Her dad never told her stories about the war, about her grandfather being the instigator. He said he was never involved in it and that any stories told by the humans who planned it would be filled with their propaganda.

No one came back from the war and so no one would ever know the truth, but the magi who were left behind to man the tethers of those who travelled told stories of their own. How every soul who crossed to the Shores of Separation was mercilessly killed in cold blood by the monsters who lived there.

The narrative twisted and changed over time to paint the humans as the peaceful party. The truth couldn't be further from that.

How is she supposed to deal with this mulchy ball of feelings? As though she's standing in the middle of a vast vertical tunnel and has three choices.

Fall down into the depths. Stay put and stop moving, or start climbing. In the back of her mind other vague pieces work to find a way to fit together.

Words have so much power. The magus managed to use them to change the perceptions of so many people for the worse. Put enough emotion behind them and words can do a great deal. It seems wrong that such a simple thing should have so much influence. She wonders now if humans were ever even ready for such a responsibility.

Words could be so many things. A comfort, a safety net, a reassurance, a weapon. The only words she can think of probably won't be a comfort to Dennira, but as the images cycle again from Annika's death to the severing of the bridges they're the only ones she can say.

She turns to Dennira, who gazes out over the island with her blindfolded eyes. For a brief moment she wonders what the pathmaster can see, recalling the flourish of colour, auras and pathways she'd seen through her eyes in the memories. Kyra swallows down the thick carpet of sadness coating her throat and takes a deep breath that hitches despite her best efforts. This catches Dennira's attention and the pathmaster goes stock still.

'I'm… I'm so sorry for what we did to you.' Then Kyra breaks. She continues to pour out her apology in a lament that shakes her core, bending at the middle as her lungs freeze for long seconds at a time. Among all of it Dennira barely moves, apart from one hand rising to sit on her chest and the other hanging loosely beside her. Kyra starts trying to pull herself together, apologising for her uncontrolled show of emotion. Dennira is so kind in her tone that Kyra nearly starts crying again.

'Thank you for your apology. It's one I never thought I'd get, but it shouldn't be your responsibility. You had nothing to do with the war.' The pathmaster places two fingers on the back of Kyra's hand and she gasps. A warmth spreads from the finger tips and travels under her skin, heating and soothing her body and heart. It's pure comfort.

'How did you do that?'

'Comforting souls is what we did. It was our duty.'

'I'm sorry for what we took from you. You say it's not my responsibility, but it is. More than I realised. The magus who lost his son… I'm sure it was my grandfather. That doesn't mean I can't acknowledge that what my kind did in the past was wrong. It was unspeakable. It should never have been allowed to happen in the first place. But the fact that my family were the ones… that my grandfather was the one who…' Kyra might be imagining it, but she's certain that Dennira's breath catches just a little.

'I never knew how much I needed the validation that the events of the war were wrong. Left here alone there was no way to work through it, with no one to be on my side.' There's such an open candor in Dennira's words. No venom, no defenses.

'It doesn't bother you? That it was my grandfather who…'

Dennira shakes her head. 'No. No matter who it was, it was their decision to do what they did. Regardless of what I said out of anger when you first arrived here, you aren't responsible for your ancestor's actions. Just like all of our kin weren't responsible for Annika's. I can tell by your reaction that you didn't know. You never met him, did you?'

'No... I. No. My dad never talks about him. About any of it. He would only ever say grandfather died in the war and that he was a cruel man. I knew my dad had a brother who died when they were both very young, but he's always been silent about it except to say that his dad didn't cope with his loss. He said his dad used to show him horrific images of his brother to try and persuade him to join the war as well. I never, ever thought it could be...' She trails off, unsure how to carry on speaking as the gears in her mind continue to turn. More and more things add up and unfold a picture of her family's history on a great mechanical map. 'That must be what caused it.'

'Caused what?'

'The rift in my family. If the man who caused the war was my grandfather, his wife was my grandmother. The lady who was here. Who spent time with you while she was in a coma. Why would dad keep all this from me?'

'They both lost a son. One of them chose hate, and the other love?'

'Can I ask... what actually happened to Joel? Why did he end up... the way he did?'

Dennira sighed and Kyra's heart missed a beat. Had she strangled the conversation by asking such a question? The pathmaster eventually spoke.

'Guiding souls has its challenges. When we tried to explain that what happened to Joel was an accident, we meant it. When your kind begin to pass away, their souls used to come here in preparation for moving on to their next life. The tethers are the link to the body. Your grandmother had one the whole time she was here, and it was strong and bright. Never faltering. That's rare, but it meant she had an amazingly strong spirit.

'The closer a person is to death, the more fragile their tether becomes. Joel was ill for a long time, but luck wasn't on his side and his spirit wasn't strong enough to weather it like your grandmother's was. We watch for the moment the tether severs. Once it's gone it shouldn't be able to reconnect except in rare circumstances. It's happened maybe a handful of times in our history. Annika even waited a little while to make sure Joel wouldn't be revived, but it seems they somehow managed to bring him back even after he should have been long dead. There's no way any of us could have known. Nothing we could have done.'

For a while, there's nothing but the lilting rhythm of the sea below them to fill the passing seconds.

'My grandmother always spoke highly of the pathmasters, always, even after Joel it seems. Dad said she became an outcast from the family and she fled with him. My grandfather's grief must have been what drove them apart.'

'It seems we both have responsibility in this then.'

Kyra notices the darker tone in Dennira's voice. 'What do you mean?'

'Your family killed my kin, but that also means I killed a member of your family.'

Kyra is slapped with a cold shock as the words hit home. Dennira had killed her grandfather, and many more people. She only now registers that she's sitting in the presence of a killer. Yet she doesn't feel fear. How is she supposed to react? She never met her grandfather, and after seeing Dennira's memories she's more glad of that than ever.

The more she thinks about it the more she recalls just how many souls had landed on the beach. Dennira dispatched most of them to protect kin who were already dead. She did it so effortlessly. Her anger had taken her over. A flare of danger tries to run wild in Kyra's body, but she takes a breath and asks herself what she knows.

Dennira threatened me when I first arrived. She bound me to a tree and left me there. She saved my life. She's taken care of me since I viewed the flame and made no move to hurt me. She acted to protect her kin, hoping that some might be alive. She's capable of violence, and dangerous magic. I do not know her, but I don't think she acted incorrectly.

'I… don't condone all the humans you killed but I feel you didn't have a choice. I saw my grandfather's behaviour first-hand. He needed help. Help he might have been able to get if he'd lived. You took that chance from him and all the humans who came here that day, but they also took from you as well. It's… not a simple situation and it doesn't change why I'm here.'

Dennira stays stoic as ever, the black strap across her eyes masking every feeling she has.

The way feels clear. Could this be a chance to forge a tentative bond of trust? Kyra has to try.

'I know what I ask now, and I know it's a lot. I don't believe it's something that can be decided in a short trip. It was arrogant of us to think we could just turn up and propose such a thing without knowing everything.

Everything always seems so much simpler when you don't know the whole story.'

'You are… surprisingly elegant-minded for someone so young.'

Kyra's mouth twitches in a fleeting smile at the compliment, and the tide of tension recedes for a moment. It lasts only a second as a nausea rolls over her from her midriff. A light flickers in her vision for several seconds and then disappears. The tether.

'How long have I been here?'

'Almost a full rotation of a human clock by now. What's wrong?'

'Nearly twelve hours? The longest we managed to sustain a tether was around twenty-four. Then dad's magic starts to falter. We agreed on eight hours to be as safe as possible. Then he was supposed to call me back. I shouldn't still be here.'

Kyra's mind flicks into high gear. Sometimes the questions are her friends, sometimes her foes. Right now they are the latter. What if the other magi found her dad?

They've been safe in their current home for a few years but all the signs are there. The signs that they are close to being found again. Dad didn't want to wait to try and contact the pathmasters. To go through the strain of uprooting themselves and building a new home and workshop yet again. The magi never stop looking.

Even now. Even thirty years after the war they still hunt Kyra's family to try and stop the spread of their true stories of the pathmasters. Eternally trying to cover their mistakes and keep history written the way they want it. If they find him, what will they do? She can't lose him.

'I have to get back. If the other magi find him and

he's trying to hold the tether he won't be able to defend himself against them. If they attack him the tether could snap.' Panic rises and bubbles, roils and rolls.

'It's alright. Take a breath or two. You can signal him like he told you and then you'll know.'

'I have to try. I have to go. Before I do, will you let me return? Can I come back once I know he's safe? Please? I don't want to give up on peace, but I know there's work to do. I want to learn more from you.

To come back and do what I can to earn your trust before I ask so boldly for peace again. Will you allow it?'

The question hangs in the air for precious seconds. Leeching them away. Frustration flashes but she can't rush Dennira. She can't demand things of her. Some questions require thought before answering, and so she waits.

CHAPTER 19

The Nethercove

Dennira isn't sure how to answer. Can she permit a human to keep returning here? To the place where they took everything from her? Part of her wants to say no and carry on living the way she's learned to live, but another part sends out a dull beacon and begs to be considered.

She's alone because she had to learn to be. She adapted, telling herself it's better this way and that she's OK with the peaceful life of a lantern keeper. That's not entirely true, though. It might be buried, further down than she realises, but the longing for company and a different life never really vanished. She just squashed it and balled it up and stuffed it into a far-flung corner of herself in order to survive.

Then there's a third part. A new part. One she'd never admit exists. One that gazes into a taken future to wonder if Kyra is anything like the daughter Dennira and Annika might have had. A part that even hopes their daughter would share some of Kyra's qualities. It creates such a clotted knot of emotions that Dennira has to take a deep breath. Why picture things that can never be?

She inspects the young girl, who's face is a melding of panic and worry, and who's question hangs in the air like a sticky spider web. Kyra is the first and only human to admit their faults. That's something worth taking a chance on.

'I would allow you to return, yes. But only you.'

Relief peeks out from under Kyra's worries and she nods, then gathers her jumper off of the ground and motions to put it on. It's time for her to go. The only other live company Dennira's known for three decades. She tells herself her reluctance would surface for any human in Kyra's situation, but she doesn't believe it.

The other humans that have accidentally washed up here over the years were likely genuine mistakes. Just lost souls spat out of the fabric between plains. Yet she didn't even give them the time of day or a single shred of kindness. A spark of shame zips around her body. The death count is high enough without her adding to it. With a jolt it hits home that in those moments she became exactly what the humans were making her out to be. A monster. A killer. Her blood runs cold, and a determination to change starts to bubble quietly in her core. To think, a teenager is the one responsible for breaking through all her carefully constructed defenses and facades.

'What was it your father said you had to do to signal him?'

'Call up the tether and then pull on it. He should feel the pressure and start reeling it in.'

Her hesitation is clear, but the motion is practiced. She closes her eyes and starts to whisper in the language of the magi. She has decent mastery over it, but Dennira supposes she's been learning it her whole life. As Kyra opens her eyes again the silver glow is brighter and flecked with shining stars. The glow outlines her body and a tether flickers into view, attached to her back. She reaches back and carefully wraps her palm around it, pulling it towards her with certainty in short, repeating motions. One, two, three. They wait. Nothing changes.

Dennira feels sympathy for Kyra. If she's unable to get home then she must know the consequence. She'll start to fade the more the tether's limit is reached. If she fades too much the tether will snap, cutting off her soul from her body. She'll die. Kyra may not realise it yet, but if her father can usually make a tether last for a full cycle of a day and it's starting to deteriorate now, then it's likely he's not maintaining the flow of magic through it. Which could mean… just about anything had happened to him.

Dennira doesn't speculate, but there must be some way she can help this girl. This family. The family that was also torn apart by the war. The family who were split by love and hate, and Kyra is the representative of love. How can she turn that away? Maybe there is space left in her heart for humans after all.

'Nothing's happening. Why isn't he calling me home?'

'Give it another try. You're a long way from your plain, he could have trouble feeling the signal.' Kyra looks like she wants to disagree. To argue that her father is too diligent to miss it, but she bites it back and focuses. More deliberate this time, and with stronger tugs. One. Two. Three. They wait again. Nothing changes… again. Kyra's hands start to shake.

'No no no something's happened to him. They've found him. They have to have found him there's no other reason he'd ignore the signal.'

She looks around. For what, Dennira doesn't know. Kyra's eyes go wide as she takes small steps in several directions only to keep returning to her original spot. She wrings her hands like wet towels that will never dry.

'Take a moment, Kyra. We can figure this out.' We? They're 'we' now? So much for not getting attached. A well-timed jingle from the bell on her staff teases her in a similar way and Dennira bites back a scoff.

'How? I don't know how to get home and all the bridges are closed. If I stay here I'll start fading and...' she can't say it. Dennira is glad she's been properly educated on the dangers of staying on a tether for too long, but that's a big burden for a teenager to bear. It means she came here knowing that there was a chance things could go wrong. That's a lot to risk for peace. An awful lot. If she can risk that to rebuild a link so utterly desecrated by the history between their two species, then Dennira can risk trying to help a human for the first time since she renounced her duty.

Kyra stops. She's completely still. Her hand moves to her waist so slowly that Dennira wonders if everything has slowed down along with it. Kyra looks down, tears threatening the surface of her eyes, and lifts the side of her blouse. There, among the landscape of her skin, is a small patch of grey. It blooms in an imperfect ink blot then stops. No bigger than a coin. It's starting. The fading is beginning. The clock just started ticking a little faster.

Kyra lets out a sigh punctuated with a tiny sob and drops her blouse and jumper again. However much Dennira wants to, she can't ignore that. If a soul is a lighthouse to predators of the sea when it's stable, then an unstable one is like the aroma of a delicious meal to a starving man. The waters already churn more deeply. Things are on the move that have slumbered and starved for too long. Or not long enough. Some that would stop at nothing for a meal dripping with the power of a human soul. Dennira doesn't want any more uninvited guests. Especially not those from the deep of the dark sea. Another jingle of the bell tinkles through Dennira's mind and scampers around until it finds the idea it was looking for.

'You're right, thank you Annika.'

Kyra frowns. 'What?'

'Annika reminded me of something. There's a way for us to check on your father. We have to get to the back of the island. It will be quicker if you let me carry you.' Dennira turns around and crouches, gesturing for Kyra to climb on to her back.

'What's at the back of the island?'

A shard of reluctance settles in Dennira's gut. She has to stop putting it off and she did promise Jennir she'd go and harvest the crystal herbs soon. With a heavy sigh she steels herself.

'I can explain on the way. We're going to the Nethercove.'

CHAPTER 20

A Separate Plain

Despite her panic and everything else, Kyra has to swallow a laugh. Seeing Dennira crouch and offer her back to be climbed on to is such a foreign concept. Such an elegant and reserved person lugging a teenager around the island in a piggyback just doesn't seem right. But it has to be done. Wherever and whatever the Nethercove is, if it will help them to check on her dad then she will happily ride the creature that came after her through the fog to get there. He should be able to hold a tether for longer, even if they did agree on eight hours. He'd never leave her with no answer. Something has happened.

With only another few moments hesitation she walks over to a very patient Dennira and clambers on to the back of her body. Just as she's lifted from the ground another small grey speck catches her attention on the back of her hand. They have to hurry.

'I will move quickly, so be sure to hold on. It won't be a comfortable ride.'

'A-alright.'

She leans into Dennira's back. The smell of rich earth fills her nose, but a hint of a calming herbal scent counteracts it. Dennira moves her silky black hair to one side and renews her grip on Kyra's legs.

'Hold this close to me.' Dennira presses her staff into Kyra's hands. She grips it tight and pulls it close to the pathmaster as requested. It hums with warmth under her palms, a strange resonance crackling through her. 'OK, here we go.'

With a power Kyra wouldn't have thought Dennira's slender legs could hold they lurch forward. Kyra bites back a yelp as they start to move faster. They leap and drop, run and swerve. The jagged terrain passes under them in a blur. Kyra pushes a cheek into the space between Dennira's shoulderblades and grips the silver staff tighter. It will be over soon. Her stomach rises into her throat and she tells herself that no, they didn't just jump off of the ridge of a cliff and they're not going to die.

She distracts herself with thoughts. They turn to her dad, hoping he hasn't been harmed by the other magi. Then to her grandfather, the man who started the culling of a whole species over the loss of one child. Kyra hasn't spent much time around children, but being a mum isn't something she's even thought about. That kind of connection with another human seems such a burden and forever binding. She remembers her own mother in great detail, her grandmother too but only from the pictures around their home. Knowing her grandmother chose love over hate makes her proud.

Grandma was put in the same situation. Both of them lost a child, but her grandfather never recovered. Never accepted it. Even used his other son. Tried to turn him to the cause of avenging his sibling by showing him horrific images of his brother's twisted body when his soul returned from the shores.

A clod of shame drops into Kyra's stomach in tandem with another lurch as they fall several feet.

Learning her own family are the cause of Dennira's pain is hard to swallow. She wishes it weren't true. That none of it had happened. Wishing something away... wasn't that the same as ignoring it, though? Saying it should never have happened doesn't change the fact that it did.

What would her dad do? If it was her who's soul was burned by the blue fire and thrown back into her body to twist and break it? Would he become like grandfather? Bent on revenge and slicked in an oil of grief too slippery for logic to take hold? No. No, there was no way. Her dad would take the same path as his own mother had done. He'd never blame someone for something that was out of their hands. He'd never take so much in return for his loss.

Then another thought crept up through the smog of fear that she was ignoring as they took a sliding skid on a narrow cliff-side path. What would she do? If her dad had been lost due to a mistake made by the pathmasters, would she still be so forgiving and eager for peace? She can't imagine it. Can't imagine him gone. A void starts to open in her chest and she shakes the thoughts away, coming full circle to worry about her dad once more.

With a final, impossible leap they spring into the air and land on a strip of beach hidden at the back of the island. Kyra shudders seeing the water so close, picturing eels slowly undulating back and forth in the shadows. Waiting. Watching.

In her confident strides Dennira takes them through a narrow valley carved into the cliff. It's only a few steps long, and then they find themselves in a kind of antechamber and a great, black crevice looms open before them. Dennira gently helps Kyra to peel herself off of her back. Dark stains mark her green jumper again and a flare of embarrassment heats her face. Dennira makes no mention of it and might have even offered a kind smile as she holds out a hand to reclaim her staff.

Kyra doesn't trust her legs much as her feet hit the sand-dusted stone. They quiver slightly as she stands, not wanting to think about the fact that she just descended a sheer cliff riding pillion on a pathmaster. It's then that it settles around her. A thickness in the air that makes it heavy. It's almost like a presence in itself. Wrapping around her not unlike the fog from the eel that hunted her. It stirs her stomach with suspicion and unease. Dennira seems to sense it.

'You can't enter this place with me. I know the air here will feel strange to you. This place is anchored here, but it isn't part of this world. It's a separate plain. If you venture in to it your tether could weaken and your fading quicken.' The information bounces off of Kyra's mind, knocking at the door of logic and being denied entry.

'There's… another world in there?' She motions to the cave.

'In a sense. A plain doesn't have to refer to an entire world, but the idea is the same on a much smaller scale.'

'Is this the place where you came to watch my grandfather after… after he threatened Annika? The place that let you watch him?'

'It is. You have a good memory now there's no memoracle lodged in there.' A wan smile passed between them.

'So… I have to stay out here?' She feels childish for casting a glance back out towards the sea. Every fibre in her body tells her to beg Dennira not to leave her alone, but she pushes it down.

'Yes, but not for long. Once I'm at the core of the Nethercove I can link to your mind and we can find your dad's lifestring.'

'Our minds can link? How?'

'They linked already back at the Ingress. It's how I shared my memories. It will be easy to reconnect if you give me permission when you feel my consciousness reach out for yours.' Kyra nods in a daze. She wants to ask what a lifestring is, but can already sense the ticking of Dennira's growing impatience mixing with her own anxiety. 'Call me back with your voice and your mind if anything unusual happens or if you feel endangered. I'll get back here as fast as I can.'

'Endangered?'

'The more you fade, the stronger the scent of your soul will be to stalking creatures.' And with that Dennira vanishes into the crevice.

'Oh… wonderful.' Kyra picks a spot next to the entrance to the Nethercove and sits down, pressing her back against the smooth rock and hugging her knees. She stares at the sliver of beach beyond, watching the water lap against the shore in the rhythm of a slow-ticking clock. 'Just wonderful.'

CHAPTER 21

Field of Skyless Stars

As Dennira enters the darkness of the cave her stomach stirs with unease. Kyra is a ticking time bomb, and the lower the timer gets, the more vulnerable she is to… things not worth considering until they have to. She has to be swift.

When was she last in this place? She can't remember. In the gloom the air changes and opens out into a large cavern that bores down into the earth below the island. A spiral path lies dormant, but with a single tap of her staff the ground illuminates and awakens the Nethercove.

Symbols trace themselves with a gentle white light that tumbles down into the depths. The path makes itself visible, resting in its circling pattern. A great, coiled serpent. The walls glitter and glisten, the light dancing off the purple crystals in slick refractions.

Dennira takes a breath as ghosts flicker from her mind out into the cave. She forgot about its beauty, but it was far more prevalent when it was also filled with her kin. There was a time when this cavern was bustling with pathmasters as they extracted minerals from the walls and checked lifestrings, or drew water from the crystal pool at its base. Now it's empty and echoing with loss.

The beauty a shade of its previous splendour.

She starts her descent, running her fingers over the sparkling grit of the minerals that sprout from the walls. She chooses some nodes of the crystal herbs to deftly pry away, stowing them in a summoned pouch. She only needs a few initially, and can come back for the rest later. The dust coats her fingers and some of the crystals glow to become lamps as she travels down, sensitive to the presence of living spirits.

The path takes her down and around, circling the colossal white crystal that sits nestled as the centrepiece of the Nethercove. It's as though the path was dug around it to excavate it like some lost relic, but it was forged by her people. The path opens out onto the smooth floor. A spacious lobby. She looks up at the dormant centrepiece and smiles at the view of twinkling minerals that bathe in the calm luminosity of the path. A field of skyless stars.

When she was younger she used to come here with Annika and simply lie on the floor at night gazing up. They would talk and pass the time, their attention wrapped around each other in fascination. They carried on the tradition for years after they became bonded. Their spirits locked together in willing entanglement from that moment.

She shakes off the memories. There is a small pool of cloudy water lapping at the base of the crystal. Ripples flowing towards it even without a wind or breath to create them. She doesn't know how deep the pool is. It's not the kind of pond you can just immerse your hooves in to cool off. She dips the bottom of her staff into the liquid and then extends the top to touch the flat, smooth surface of the grand structure. The ripples begin to flow outwards instead, and the blemishes on the surface of the water and the crystal itself roll away. Grey clouds disintegrating after a storm to leave only clear skies. The mineral seems to turn to glass that glints with silver and above her they appear in the thousands.

Gossamer strings languish in shoals in every inch of the cave. Lifestrings. Golden and fragile, moving in unflustered waves and floating effortlessly. There are too many to count, sentient threads weaving around each other. Part of some overarching tapestry that no one will ever make sense of. She could be lying on the ocean floor staring up at the sky through the undulating surface far above. Docile fish minding their own business around a coral reef of crystal. Still, she has a task to complete.

She sends her consciousness out along the connection she forged with Kyra at the Ingress and tries not to startle her too much. She doesn't know how successful she is as Kyra's thoughts jump and surge at her presence.

'Kyra. I need you to think of your father. It will help me find what I need to see him on the human plain.'

'Um… OK. Just think of him?'

'Just picture him, yes. Thank you.'

There's a hesitancy in Kyra's thoughts as she tries to separate her worries from her memories. Colours dance together to show the smiling, but tired, face of a man who has a kind and knowledgeable feel about him. He looks like any other human. Some of the magi who came to siege the shores had donned themselves in ornate robes and other such ridiculous garbs, but Kyra's father simply wears jeans and a t-shirt. His smile is broad and warm, his brown skin clearly passed down in strong part to Kyra herself. His hair is close cut at the back and sides, but locs cover the top of his scalp and they're pulled back into a ponytail.

Her eyes are also his, dark with a hint of mischief and curiosity. Dennira finds herself drawn to him, believing Kyra completely when she says he wants nothing but peace. There's a sincerity there that's reflected in his daughter. She holds the image central in her mind and touches the curved crook of her staff to her own forehead, pulling out a white string.

It curls itself around the staff and she offers it to the crystal which consumes it. Now she waits and looks up among the shoals of lifestrings. A single string gleams and straightens, isolating itself from the meandering movements of its peers. Then it slackens, floating down in slow, feathery arcs, and comes to rest in front of the glass crystal. It fuses with the surface temporarily and images twist into being on the gigantic earthen pillar.

The man from Kyra's thoughts is there, but he's splayed on a wooden floor, various things strewn about him. He doesn't move, but his lifestring wouldn't have answered the call if he was dead. The door in the background is ajar, and the tether protruding from his palm flickers dangerously. A puffy welt, scored with a ragged cut, marks the ridge of his forehead above one eye. A scribbled letter lies next to his face, but she can't make it out. A summons, perhaps. A threat? He can't call Kyra home in that state. There's no way to wake him from this plain. The crystal only shows images, it doesn't create functional connections.

Kyra's already fading, her soul is losing its colour.

Losing its connection to the plain where her body lives. If she can't be called back she'll end up lost in the soul belt. A dangerous place for an untethered spirit. She's rotting. Expiring. The soul needs a body to live and vice versa. Thinking about it won't help much.

First, she has to tell Kyra that her worries are founded after all. That her father has likely been attacked by the magi.

CHAPTER 22

Overstayed Her Welcome

Kyra shivers against another breath of sour wind and huddles her legs tighter to her chest. She keeps her ears pricked for further questions from Dennira, then shakes her head at herself wondering what good it will do listening externally for an internal voice. She's heard nothing since Dennira asked her to think of her dad. Hopefully her images of him did the trick. When will she be back?

One foot taps a quick rhythm on the sand-strewn stone. Dad always said she had a restless leg. Ceaselessly bobbing up and down no matter how casually she sits. The more bothered she is by something, the worse the bobbing gets, but she doesn't like being out here alone. Dennira hasn't even said how long she'll be.

In that moment, Kyra just wants to be back at home. She has a full complement of ammunition packed full of questions that her dad will be made to answer. All the stuff he kept back. About the war, about her grandfather. She's old enough to have difficult conversations. More than old enough. If he's going to send her on missions, she needs to be better armed with the facts.

Yet she can't be too angry with him, not really. The heat of her own hurt eases off a little. He's always struggled to talk about his family no matter how many questions she asked as a child. Every time he'd shut down in some way, disappearing inside himself to a place that haunted his eyes and harrowed his soul. The memories took part of him away from her, so eventually she stopped asking.

Yes, it would have been helpful to know, but maybe… just maybe she shouldn't put her own demand for information above her dad's trauma and hurt.

She'll ask her questions. She'll ask them gently and with care, and let him know that he isn't alone and that she's there to listen. She's his daughter. It's her job.

All the signs are there that she's overstayed her welcome on this plain. Everything her dad told her to watch out for. A sour smell on the wind, the grey freckling of monocolour on her skin. A light nausea. It's all starting. Then the wind picks up. Stirs in unusual ways. It brings more than the unpleasant smell, it brings the thick feeling of ichor. Clotting in clouds around her as though sensing her. Smelling her and reporting back.

Out near the sea, the water level seems higher. It's moving in a different way. Swirling and flowing forward, crawling up the beach. It's not the sea. It's the fog. Another eel?

'Dennira!' Her call echoes around her in the small inlet and staggers down into the cave. Kyra leaps to her feet and presses her back against the cliff. There's nowhere to go as the dark mist rolls around, searching for the source of the scent. Dennira said that didn't she? That the longer Kyra stays here and the more she deteriorates, the stronger her scent becomes? Something wants to devour her. To take her for its prey.

Her stomach becomes ten times longer and she feels the drop. Watching for flickering figures stretching out of the writhing shadows.

In a flurry Dennira leaps out of the cave and Kyra bites her tongue in surprise, letting out a little squeak.

'What happened? You sounded frightened.'

Kyra can only point towards the short path back to the beach. As Dennira turns to follow her pointing finger her eyebrows vanish beneath her blindfold.

'Is it the same creature as before?' Kyra mumbles in a clumsy way as her tongue pulses from the bite.

'No. It's a different creature. They all use the same kind of fog to cast their senses out on land but this one is... not the same. It is... older.'

As a curtain of silence descends around Dennira's puzzling statements a bolt shoots through Kyra and she grabs Dennira's forearm.

'Dad! What's happened to dad, did you see him?' Dennira takes Kyra's hand but doesn't patronise her.

'It's as you feared. It looks like he's been attacked but he didn't seem too badly injured. The room was a mess, they seem to have been looking for something.'

Kyra nods with an odd mix of certainty and panic. 'They must want the research notes for these tethers we use. They're different to the ones used in the war. More sustainable and stronger, and they use a better energy. That's why they won't kill us, only inconvenience us. If they can't find the notes we are the only ones who know the magic. What can we do? I have to get back.'

This time Kyra's not shivering because of the cold. She knew the magi would come soon. They'd almost found them a few weeks back. She tried to tell her dad that they weren't safe enough to try the crossing in their situation. Using the tether magic would only alert the magi more, but he didn't want to wait again. More years with the bridges still closed. More souls turning to dust instead of being allowed their walk to another life and world. He won't forgive himself if he lets her tether break. She knows that for certain.

'I will have to send you home. Ever since I destroyed the bridges these shores are not so well protected. Either way, we have to get away from the beach and go inland.'

'How can you send me home, I thought it was impossible?'

Dennira sighs. Her indecision almost visible in a quaking aura around her. Whatever she's decided is something that she's reluctant to do.

'I can reforge the connection through one bridge. Just one. I wouldn't do it unless there was no other choice. It's a taxing process to repair a broken vow of duty. I'm not ready for it, but I can build a one-way bridge to send you home. It won't let any others through, but it will make the island vulnerable for a while.'

'I don't want to bring danger to the island.'

'You already have.' The words cut Kyra, until Dennira added a few more. 'But you also brought me sincerity. Kindness. Willingness to learn the truth and the start of some small validation for my pain. You are the first human to offer such a thing. I can, therefore, offer something back in return as well.'

With a swift and graceful movement she forces her staff into the sky after balancing the bottom of it in her palm. It rises so high and so fast that Kyra's neck strains to follow it and she has to look down again. A beautiful call goes out like a beacon and tiny wisps of blue flame skitter in all directions. After mere seconds they return, each with slightly different notes as they rejoin the main source of the fire. When the staff returns to her hand the pathmaster listens with her face turned up to the sky. Then she crouches down in front of Kyra, who can't help but flinch. Not this again.

'Annika called back the strongest, that means the bridge near her is the safest. We have to go now. I'll keep you safe.'

'Can't… can't you fly? Like in the memories? I mean can't I just run alongside you…'

'You wouldn't be able to keep up, unless you're hiding a pair of very strong animal legs under those jeans. And no, I can't fly again. We only get to do that once, and once alone. In dire need. We still have a bit of time. Trust me.'

Kyra climbs onto Dennira's back for what she hopes is the last time, and once again she holds the staff tight for Dennira as she links the crooks of her elbows under Kyra's knees. 'OK, we're going back up.' Kyra grits her teeth and gasps through them as Dennira leaps into motion, taking the non-existent path back up the grand and jutting mound at the back of the island.

CHAPTER 23

Duty Long Renounced

Dennira clings to Kyra's legs during their rough re-ascension of the cliffs, wary of how fast she's moving and how much power she's forcing into her leaps. They have to move fast. Kyra has buried her face into the back of Dennira's robes again and that's probably for the best. If she looks down now she'll see them perched on an impossibly thin ledge that Dennira's hooves navigate with a confidence only the animal part of her can execute. Instinct has to lead in situations like these.

As they climb, Dennira gets a strange and foreboding sense of déjà vu. It didn't escape her notice that the lanterns called back to say the gate that's the safest right now is the bridge where Joel was snatched back to his world.

It isn't possible for the same thing to happen again. Kyra is still attached to her body and she isn't crossing to a further world, just going back to her own. Everything will be fine. It will be fine.

If Kyra can feel the hammering of Dennira's heart, hopefully she'll put it down to the effort of carrying her while she climbs. In truth Dennira is barely breaking a sweat. Her powerful legs mean she can jump while holding almost three times her weight and hardly notice.

Her distress is from her nervousness. The call to pick up her duty again has come knocking once or twice in the thirty years since the war. She never gave into it, and after a while she worried she'd lost her ability to even call to and command the bridges anymore. They are about to find out if that's true or not.

As they make it to the top Dennira lets Kyra get down. Despite doing none of the work Kyra's legs are shaking and her steps uncertain. It must have been a little disorienting and uncomfy for her, but Dennira isn't made to offer piggybacks to teenagers and time is of the essence. She allows a few seconds for the girl to catch her breath and steady herself.

'Follow me, the gate is over here.' Kyra follows, her pallor looking sickly, and as they pass the lantern Dennira's bell tinkles in encouragement. Annika telling her that she's doing the right thing. Whether she's right or not is another matter. They walk past Annika's lantern, past the entrance to Dennira's home and a short walk brings them to the western edge of the cliff where two dilapidated columns sit at the end of a wide overhang. They've been claimed by nature over time and sport blotches of moss and small tangles of delicate plants. It's been so long since they've been active, what if they don't answer her call?

'This bridge… isn't it…' Kyra doesn't finish her question. That's a rarity. She doesn't miss much, she knows this is Joel's bridge too. Dennira takes a look down to the beach from their vantage point and sees just how far the fog has spread. It's covering every inch of sand and is starting to creep inland. Something with a consciousness this vast is much bigger than a covet eel.

'What's wrong?'

'Nothing, we are safe up here. The fog won't reach.'

'What's down there?' Kyra moves towards the edge, intending to peer down, and Dennira stops her with the length of her staff.

'It's best not to look. We have to repair the gate and get you home.' Kyra's eyes burn with determination. The grey patches on her skin are more widespread now, and are growing. 'Step back a little, please.' Kyra obliges and Dennira's heart canters. It's time to learn whether she can still connect to the magic of her own plain. The magic of her duty long renounced.

She takes a deep breath, flinching at the acrid tang in the air and still trying to figure out which creature is sniffing around her island. She needs focus to do this, though. She feels like she's intruding on herself. Reaching deep within to pull buried secrets loose like hidden, stubborn weeds. Clearing the debris off her slate. Excavating it from under a choking sheen of dust. She knocks on the door of her core and is surprised to find she's allowed entry with relative ease. Only the slightest resistance and flicker of uncertainty greets her. Then her magic flows around her as though she's used it every day.

Her staff knows the movements through its own memory of what it was created to do. The deep-set ache that became so ingrained in Dennira day after day that she simply learned to live with it howls in triumph. It reaches out with grasping hands for the tendrils of their long-lost magic and hungrily binds itself to them. Tying off the tatters that hung loose for thirty years, revitalising the magic circuits that have long sat dull and colourless within her.

She's home again. Where she belongs. It thrums through her body, awakening her slumbering energies. Dennira hadn't realised how flat, how one-dimensional she's become.

How cold and desolate without her magic. Without her duty. She bites back an elated smile. One at a time her staff acts out the required positions and when she stamps its base on the rocky ground in front of the crumbling gates the tired stones leap to life and rebuild their original structure. The plants and moss are cleared away, the torches on each pillar straighten, ready to receive the warmth of the blue flames. A soft 'wow' escapes Kyra's lips behind her as the pillars are remade. Their ornate inscriptions are bolstered as the dust clears and they look brand new again.

A pressure that Kyra won't be able to feel settles into place between the two columns of stone. The weight of other worlds pressing against the barrier. The connection is reforged. She always imagined that she lost her abilities the day she broke her vow. A tightness filled with pride and apprehension weaves around her ribs. A missing piece slots gently back into place. If she were to take off her blindfold, would she see everything she used to see? Since covering her eyes she assumed the colours had died with her duty. Not yet though, she can't afford to be overwhelmed.

'Is it fixed?'

Dennira keeps forgetting Kyra is there. She's too swept up in the whirlwind of emotions storming through her. A happiness that she didn't expect, a sense of belonging and purpose returning to her. The sense that she's no longer alone somehow, even though nothing yet everything has just changed. There's a prickle of suspicion that it's somehow all a cruel lie.

'It is, it's ready.'

'Dad once said that pathmasters can't control where a bridge goes. Is that true?' A light sheen of sweat shines on the teenager's forehead.

'It is true, but only when a soul is no longer attached to its body. You still have a connection to your original world and to a living body, so I can use that information to link the bridge to the correct world. No bridge only leads to one place. When a soul isn't anchored, it chooses its own destination.'

'So you can make bridges that go anywhere if you want?'

'We could. There are many worlds anchored to this island and pathmasters would often go and visit other places sometimes. Whether for research into new magics or uses for herbs, or just to explore. We are naturally curious species and value knowledge.'

'Did you… have you ever considered going to another world? Starting again somewhere new?'

Dennira turns her head to look at Kyra after this question and she already lowers her eyes in apology as though she's trespassed. Yet, Dennira finds she doesn't mind at all. The gates give off a soft glow at the top as they await their dose of flame from her staff.

'I thought of it. Many times I'd hoped that some of our kind had been off visiting other worlds when the war reached its climax. Then I remember that we'd all agreed not to travel while we believed there was a looming threat from your world so that we could protect each other. Those who were travelling at the time felt the call to come home. I ran from gate to broken gate sometimes in the first years after the war ended, hoping to hear someone knocking on the other side of them, but it was all futile. I did wonder about leaving, but if I left this island behind the lanterns would burn out. I am bound to this place with more than just my memories. I am the last of my kind. I belong here in our place of origin to protect it.'

'I can't imagine how lonely you must have been all this time.' There it is, another validation.

Another person recognising what she's been through and not just telling her everything will be OK, or that she deserves the fate she wrought. A pang shoots across Dennira's middle. To hear someone else say it makes it hit home more. Makes it more real. When you adapt you often cover the grief with the coping, until someone else comes and rips off the mask you've made for yourself. Initially it hurts, but then the comfort of someone reaching out makes a small start in repairing the damage.

'I was. I truly was. But I'm glad I waited here.'

'You are?'

'Yes. Had I left this plain for another, I would not have met you, Kyra. I wouldn't have the chance to be redeemed from becoming what the magis' stories have turned me into in the minds of so many others over time. I had become the monster they spoke of until you came here and woke me from my bitter grief. I do hope you will keep your promise to return. We have much to discuss.'

Dennira fights back a smile at the baffled look on Kyra's face. Even more so as she blushes when Dennira offers a low and humble bow towards her. Her jaw works, probably trying to think what to say, but Dennira shakes her head. 'You don't have to reply, but now we have to get you home. Think of your world, and your wish to return to it, and then approach the gates.'

CHAPTER 24

Think of Home

A flush of embarrassment and happiness rises in Kyra on hearing Dennira's words. The more time she's spent on the island, the more Dennira has opened up. They've managed to create the start of a small bond even in the wreckage of the history between their species. It fills her up, flowing into every inch of her and warming her skin and her core. Hope. Hope for rebuilding the link between their worlds.

She has no idea what to say, but as Dennira rightly said there's no time to continue the discussion. Kyra nods once, walking up to the space between the two pillars, and thinks of home. Of the sun on her face and the smell of the rain. Of the comfort of her home and the warmth of her dad's presence nearby. She lets her memories roll forward and wishes with all her heart to go back.

Dennira moves behind her and one by one touches her staff to the torches on either side. The fire takes instantly as though the receptacles were already warm and waiting with eager arms to embrace the dancing blue flames. A flash of light rushes past Kyra and up into the sky and they both watch it go.

Kyra's mouth drops and hangs open as the belt of stars above them comes to life and the souls start falling towards the island, their soft light unfolding into glowing transparent slats that lay themselves in front of her. Ropes snake out of the pillars and wind around each other and the slats to tie them together. It all extends out across the sea, high above the surface of the water, and rolls out to make a bridge that has no end that she can see.

A current begins to flow along the channel of the bridge, calling to Kyra and beckoning her out on to the beautiful structure. She looks back at Dennira in her uncertainty. Questions queuing up. Pretty though it is, she still can't shake the feeling of walking off the edge of a plank and plummeting down into the viscous water below.

'It is safe. I promise you. The bridge will take you home. I hope your father recovers quickly and that you find him otherwise unharmed.' Words stick in Kyra's throat and she can't suppress the impulse. She takes two quick, long steps and throws her arms around Dennira's waist. Dennira gasps and turns stock still, but Kyra doesn't care. She needed to do it in the absence of being able to form the words to say thank you. To her surprise, Dennira returns the embrace in a cautious but genuine way. 'Come now. You have to go back. I'll wait for you.'

Kyra takes in the pathmaster's face once more and sees the subtle smile playing on her lips.

'I'll be back soon. Thank you, Dennira.'

Without another glance she peels herself away, takes a deep breath, and before she can even question or think about it steps foot on the magic bridge that was summoned from the sky.

The bridge doesn't sway or shudder under her steps

like she expects. Her foot lands with a solid dull thud as though she's walking on a laminated floor. She instantly feels safe and keeps the cycle going. One foot in front of the other. While the bridge seems endless she knows that she'll cross back over to her own world at some point if she can just keep walking.

Dennira's gaze watches her back and that only adds to the reassurance as she gets further and further away from the island. Then Kyra makes a mistake. She looks down. Then back. Her steps slow but don't stop. What is that? The fog has covered every inch of the beach. It's starting to creep up onto the mainland, crawling like clawing fingers scraping their way through the soil. Searching. Hunting. Will Dennira be alright?

The island looks so small behind her, but the flashing catches her attention. All across the island from the bulbous, rocky back to the smoother plain of the front the blue glow of the lanterns are blaring bright and then fading and repeating. She can't help but feel it's some kind of warning. Stop. Stop. Stop. Or perhaps they're just bidding her farewell. Dennira still watches, that slight smile on her face. If something is wrong, surely she'll let her know?

Kyra shakes off the uncertain churning that unsettles her stomach and keeps walking, trying not to look down at the inky darkness of the sea below. Think of home. Think of dad. He needs you. She trains her eyes forward just in time to miss the colossal shadow that passes through the water under the bridge beneath her.

CHAPTER 25

When You Come Back

A strange bundle of feelings vie for importance as Dennira watches Kyra walk further and further away. A hesitant warning chimes as the lanterns flash, but she can't hear what they're trying to say. Their voices are drowned out by a rising, sneaking tide of unexpected sadness. Her only company in three decades is leaving. Silence chimes in her ears and for a moment she can't ever go back to it. The emptiness. The quiet. It takes all her restraint not to reach a hand out to beckon the teenager back. The resonance from her energy fizzling out where as only minutes ago the island was crackling with it. When calm tears brim up behind her blindfold Dennira also misses the passing of the colossal shadow, but she senses its power as it passes by and slinks off in a wide curve around the island.

The volume of its power forces her to take a step backwards, and suddenly all the chimes of the lanterns are in her ears and the bell on her staff rings in panic. It's malicious. Hungry. Desperate.

'No it can't be. Why this creature? One hasn't been here for over a century.' The bridge connections used to afford the island a net of protections, with only the most desperate creatures trying their luck on the shores.

Hoping to snatch a human soul away. The pathmasters never let that happen. They were guardians and it was their job to protect the souls until they crossed their bridges.

This creature rarely needs to surface. One soul can sustain it for decades. As if to confirm her rippling dread, the water around the flat curve of the island rises with the pressure of the creature beneath gathering speed. It turns and keeps turning, gradually altering its course and tracking… straight for the bridge. It must have circled to gain momentum which means… no, it can't. 'A soul urchin. And it's going to jump.' Her mouth goes dry in a flash.

Soul urchins are some of the oldest creatures that lurk in the depths of the seas. Before the pathmasters took up the Shores of Separation as their home and blocked their path, disconnected souls would be left to fend for themselves against all manner of otherworldly fiends. So the elder used to say.

Many would find themselves snatched from the beaches or paralysed by the urchin's smoke inland, dragged away by stinging tentacles. Many creatures fled to other plains in the absence of prey. The sea is a maze of plains all by itself and some of its inhabitants need no bridges to cross between them.

Images of Joel turning with those wide eyes come back to Dennira and make the panic rise faster than she can handle. It bursts out of her as a desperate shout of Kyra's name, one she sends across the mental link between them as well.

It may have been a little too strong, but Dennira doesn't care right now. She has to get Kyra off the bridge.

She has to get her back to the island. She has to keep her safe.

The shout reaches Kyra and she turns. Her eyes wide just like Joel's had been. No. No, she won't let this happen again. For a terrifying moment Annika is standing beside her clear as day, her beautiful face twisted with horror as she turns her gaze out over the bridge. Then she's gone again, the bell tinkling wildly.

'Kyra, come back! Get off the bridge, now!'

Kyra turns her head to search the sea and sees the growing mound of water in the distance gathering speed towards her. She staggers back, then sideways, taking unco-ordinated steps and nearly tripping over herself. She's unable to take her eyes off the advancing creature even though she can't see its form. Just the size of the shadow beneath the water. She won't make it. She's too slow.

Dennira's mind races in time with her heart rate which tries to beat with every rhythm at once. What should she do? Pathmasters aren't supposed to interfere with crossings. They aren't meant to step on the bridges. But this isn't a regular crossing. It's a returning. She can't reach for her wings. She used the invocation already during the war. Even if she could summon them again she'd be no use to anyone once they'd dissipated. A fever had consumed her for days the last time. The possibility of death had seemed very real as she'd lain among the ruins of her home and life.

Despite her powerful legs she knows she isn't fast enough. She needs help, and there's only one place she can ask for it. She throws her staff into the air and calls out in the language of her kin, pleading for their help.

159

Perhaps they could lend speed to her movements or somehow bring Kyra back off of the bridge. She has no idea what to expect, what her kin can even do in such a reduced form as mere lantern-light. All the lanterns shine bright enough to light the whole island in their initial response and the flames soar like arrows towards their target of Dennira's staff.

'Help me, my kin. Help me to save my hope for the future.'

The flames collate around the staff and then leap to engulf Dennira. Kyra is still stumbling back towards the island, tears streaking down her face. The flame doesn't burn, it embraces. It shines. And from the sky comes a swarm of golden-threaded moths. Hundreds of them. Drawn to the blue beacon Dennira has become. They gather at her back and meld together as she watches in awe. She can't use the wings she called upon to help to revoke her vow, but now new ones are crafted for her and they unfurl from her back wreathed in the spirits of all those who wish to help lift her.

They glitter with gold just like the moths who mixed together to make them. Her throat tightens. Maybe she is right afterall. Maybe they do hold the essence of her kin and take them on new adventures as she imagined. Now they lend their power back to her, to give her speed and strength as she leaps high into the air and arcs towards the spot on the bridge where Kyra tries to start running.

The mound of water breaks with a clattering splash and the soul urchin aims for the bridge. Jumping high and opening its fine-toothed jaw, angling to cover the bridge with its maw. Its tendrils flail with excitement, wriggling out to try and grip the bridge and paralyse its prey.

Dennira urges herself forward faster, the song of her kin roaring around her, and grabs Kyra by the waist as she screams in the face of the twisted creature that closes in on her. Its spines collapse back against its dark skin to give it more speed. Wherever its eyes are Dennira can't make them out. She lands harshly on the glowing slats and immediately pushes off again, aided by the power of her kins' spirits. Kyra is yanked with her, lifted with another scream and clinging to the pathmaster, her face buried in Dennira's neck.

The urchin crashes into the bridge and snaps straight through it with its teeth. An echoing, splintering nest of cracks bounces and ripples through the air. Only magic older than the shores themselves can break a spirit bridge. This urchin must be ancient.

It slaps back into the water with the crumbling debris of the bridge it destroyed. A guttural, wet roar breaks free of its non-existent face. It's not happy. Its first meal in who knows how long snatched away right from under its keen hunter's nose. It won't give up that easily. The spray from the impact plumes chaotically as it is re-swallowed by the water and it thrashes in anger. Swathes of disturbed sea batter the beaches. There is no time to watch it curse her.

Dennira shoots through the air, cradling Kyra who sobs in between hitching breaths and shivers in her arms. She needs to go home. Now. She'll make a new bridge for her, a new way to send her home.

Below them another bellow rips through the air, pushing the fog away in a force of livid malice.

The surface of the water breaks once more and delivers the urchin on to the beach. Unlike the eel, it isn't swift on land. Its dangerous bulk too heavy to move with any grace. It cracks its tendrils at the sand like whips and they stick. Ice picks in the earth. Beginning the process of dragging itself towards its prey.

Dennira scours for a good place to land, taking guidance from her kin. Her heart pulses with such joy to feel like she's among them all again. She feels their love, their presence, their urgency. Their promise of protection. The urchin screeches, felling trees and leaving craters and trenches in its wake as it traverses the island. Whipped into a frenzy by Kyra's scent. Dennira holds her closer, telling her not to look.

She lands hard enough to crack the ground beneath her hooves in the centre of the ruined settlement, and a circle draws itself beneath her. Its inscriptions glow and join together and a warm, comforting wind rises up from the newly created insignia.

Even though the urchin isn't swift, it isn't exactly slow either. Its stinging threads and wildly gnashing teeth echo through the trees around them. Dennira lets Kyra go, placing her on the ground with her back to the approaching urchin. The girl flinches and trembles with every snap of a tree, or every wet drag of its bulbous body along the earth.

'Look at me, Kyra. Drown out the creature. You don't need to worry about it. You're safe. You're going home.'

'What about you, if that thing gets here how will you-' another tree groans and splinters, a huff of breath flinging debris from the forest towards them.

'Look at me. Think of home. You can do this, and I'll do the rest.'

Kyra does as she's asked, and looks directly at Dennira. A flare of determination steeling her against the commotion behind them. It's true, the creature is almost upon them. But Kyra will make it home safely. Of that there is no question. If only there was a minute more. Just a minute more to focus. What a time to be rusty.

Dennira takes Kyra's hands and the girl starts to rise into the air, face wide with surprise and even a little wonder manages to surface. As if in answer to Dennira's previous plea, her wings detach and remould themselves into the hundreds of golden moths that came to her aid. They flutter about her, moving towards the forest in a murmuration. They form a barrier at the treeline, shielding both Dennira and Kyra from the blasts of debris.

Then, as Dennira continues to guide Kyra into the air she gasps. Her heart leaping in grief and gladness. The moths each project a figure. A protective barrier of her kin block the urchin's way. Their forms flickering but clear enough to see. All her kin smile at her, their magic cutting off the urchin's path. It hurls its whips against it and the glowing wall blocking its way booms like a gong with each hit.

At the forefront, the very centre of the line of protectors, is Annika. Dennira's gut twists with longing and her breath hitches. Annika smiles. That wonderful knowing smile. One full of love and pride. One full of permission. Permission to let go. To move on. To live again. Forever entwined. Forever bonded.

Her kin are buying her time, she won't waste it.

Dennira guides Kyra higher and her blindfold disintegrates. A curtain of colours bursts into her vision. All the things she couldn't see or read with her eyes covered return. The things she didn't want to see that belonged to her duty. The life-force of every being radiates in a rainbow of light. She's lived in monochrome for so long she's forgotten the beauty of her power. Kyra's aura is a pure gold, flecked with the colours of fear and amazement, and a sadness that Dennira shares. She sees her eyes reflected in Kyra's and they hold her own personal field of stars again, as though a soul belt has been painted across her irises. Dennira finally feels whole again.

Kyra grips her outstretched hand tighter as she rises an inch at a time.

'It's safe to let go, I promise you. You'll be taken home.'

'What's happening? Your eyes. The wings. How will you fight the creature?'

'Save the questions for later, I'll tell you when you come back.'

Kyra nods and for the first time in three decades Dennira's face lights up with a full and genuine smile as the teenage girl is carried away.

EPILOGUE

See the World Anew

'Please? Come on there must be more to it than that, it can't end there!' Kyra sits up and moves to her knees, urging Dennira to continue the tale.

Dennira can only laugh. 'That's the end of the story. You've bled me dry of every tale about my kind in the history of the species. There's nothing else to tell.'

'I don't believe you. Millenniums of history and that can't be all the stories.'

'You're like a sponge. Will you ever stop absorbing things?'

'Nope, never!' They both laugh and Dennira gets up to clean her hands in the fountain at the centre of the settlement. It's in much better shape than when Kyra first came here. The fountain works, the gentle ripple of the water a welcome and relaxing sound in the peaceful atmosphere of the island. The houses aren't all rebuilt, but the rubble around them has been cleared and the nature tamed a little. Kyra joins Dennira at the fountain where she's helping to grind and prepare some herbs.

Kyra really is a sponge for knowledge. She retains and uses it well, learns fast and improvises even faster. Her visits are becoming more frequent, and she's growing into herself more with every month that passes.

Dennira feels an odd kind of maternal pride for her. If her and Annika were ever going to have a child, she could only hope they would have been something like Kyra.

Above them a grand bridge crowns the island, leading from the top of the cliff where Dennira lives and stretching out into the unknown distance. One tether to the human world has been restored, but it isn't open yet. Kyra came back, but hasn't even mentioned reopening the gates.

Has it really been almost a year? A year since Kyra first landed on the shores. Since Dennira sent her home and with the last of the light of her kin banished the soul urchin back to the sea. A year since she tore across the island to the Nethercove to check Kyra made it home safely. She had and she helped her dad, who wasn't seriously injured, to recover. Their notes on their new soul tether magic hadn't been found or taken. Since then, the gears of change have starting turning. Slowly. Painfully so, but turning nonetheless.

Kyra and her father agreed to meet the other magi, but on the condition that they listen. Truly listen, to the story Kyra had to tell. Where she'd been, the things she'd seen. It's a slow process and one that won't be settled overnight, even now they continue to come up against those whose minds won't be so easily changed about the true events of the war. But knowledge is helping to set things right. Dennira's story is being shared. Fault recognised on both sides. The teachings of Kyra's grandmother regaining their power and positive influence, coupled and strengthened with Kyra's own.

They promised to share their soul tether knowledge, but only once the last traces of their family's false propaganda has vanished from the world of the magi. That's a long way off, but at least they've made a start.

Dennira can say with absolute certainty that she trusts Kyra more than any human she has before. Things are looking up, the dead weight of loneliness made lighter by the girl's frequent visits. The wheels of tradition are changed, but still turning, as Dennira passes down knowledge she thought would otherwise die with her as the last of her species.

They sit on the side of the fountain and look up at the bridge.

'Do you think, when we eventually reach that point, that you'll be OK managing all the souls alone?' Kyra is genuinely concerned. Many of their talks centre around how one pathmaster could manage every crossing. It had been a lot of work even when there were hundreds. It isn't really possible for one to do everything unless they change the way the system works. The question is how they can make that happen.

'I'm still not sure. It's a lot. I don't know if I have the power to do it all.'

'I don't doubt you, we just need to figure it out. I wish I could do more to help.'

Dennira smiles. 'I've been waiting for you to say that.'

Kyra turns, puzzled, with a curious glint in her eye. 'You have?'

'Wait here.'

Dennira walks over to one of the houses they managed to rebuild and disappears inside for a few seconds. When she returns she's holding a second staff. Kyra meets her in the middle of the courtyard and stares at it with wonder. It's made of ivory, carved with intricate symbols. It has its own crook, though no bell. It hums as Dennira places it into Kyra's hands.

'What's this? Where did it come from?'

'I made it from my antlers. I kept them since the war, and never could let them go. I know now why it was that I couldn't part with them. They were meant for you. To become your staff. So that I can make this offer to you now.'

'Dennira it's… beautiful. But how can I accept this? What can I use it for?'

'Always asking questions when you're about to get the answers anyway.' Dennira lifts Kyra's chin with a finger so their eyes meet and Kyra picks up on the sincerity there. 'You were the spark of peace in a suffocating smog of hate. You reached out and did not bring your bias with you. You were open to the truth. My truth. And you did not deny it. You listened instead. You tried to understand. For that I can only offer you one thing. This staff, and the offer of making you an honorary pathmaster.'

'An honorary… can humans even…' Kyra gawps and Dennira beams.

'It is not something that's ever been offered before. It's a new way forward. I'll have no blood children to pass my power to, and it's true that ordinary humans wouldn't be able to wield or learn such magic. But you're a magus, so I believe you'll be able to learn. That you can help us find a new way. A brand new path made of the essence of both our worlds and magics.

'You were the true bridge between your world and mine, not me. The shores let you through. They brought you here. They see and feel something in you that is neither common nor ordinary. There will always be a place for you here. You will have all the powers and knowledge of my kin if you wish, because I now count you among them, if you'll agree?'

Kyra nods with tears brimming and spilling on to her cheeks. Dennira touches the crook of Kyra's staff briefly to her own and passes part of the flame to it. The staff bursts with energy and then settles to a blue glow. A blanket of stars manifests in Kyra's eyes and she takes in the world with her new vision. A myriad of colours will unfurl and burst into view. Painting the world with a new palette. A new meaning.

A new beginning.

This time it's the pathmaster who opens her arms to welcome Kyra into an embrace. This girl will have to learn to see the world anew again, but who better to teach her that than Dennira?

Acknowledgements

I've been very lucky in the amount of support I've received over the journey of becoming the person and writer I am now, and all of that tremendous support has helped me get to this point where I'm releasing my own fantasy works. There are so many folks I could thank here, but some can't go without mention.

My older sister, Kay, who has always shown an interest in my writing and let me waffle on for hours about all the stories I want to bring to life.

My partner James, for your support in not just writing but everything I try and put my mind to.

My amazing cover artist, Eli, who always seems to be able to reach into my mind and pick out the exact thing I try to describe. I'm so proud to have your art on the outside of my works.

The community of the Writer's Block Discord server. A place that's become my second home, and that's filled with so many wonderful, wholesome people that you can't help but feel encouraged and motivated to continue with your projects, and supported when you have to set things aside.

My beta readers, you all know who you are! Without your interest, enthusiasm, patience and critique this story wouldn't exist in its current form.

And finally to you, reader. I'll forever be grateful for the fact that you took the time and a chance on reading this story.

Next project coming early 2023
on Royal Road!

Dreamsmiths

A fantasy novel

www.royalroad.com/profile/249195
/fictions

Printed in Great Britain
by Amazon